CELESTIAL

MATE

CELESTION WOLVES BOOK 2

CHARLENE PENDER

KISSMANN BOOKS

Book Cover by Sweet n' Spicy Designs

Interior Wolf Art by Etheric Tales

Proofreading by K. Ward

ISBN-13 (print): 978-1-7382572-2-5

ISBN 13 (eBook): 978-1-7382572-1-8

ALSO BY CHARLENE PENDER

Celestion Wolves series
An Alien Romance series

Celestial Wolves

Celestial Rescue *(short story – included in Tales of Howloween)*

Celestial Mate

Four Snakes of Vancity series
A Mafia Romance series

A Python for Christmas *(short story)*

Other:

Tales of Howloween

For all those who never wanted to fall in love

LISA

DAY 3

"*It's payday, ladies!*"

I could hear the grin in Allison's voice, hidden behind her face shield as the drill's laser finished cutting into the rock. As the machine quieted and the glow from the laser subsided, I looked over her shoulder. Allison lifted her mask, and sure enough, an enormous grin was plastered on her face. I mirrored it as I stared at the large vein of alvionite we'd found. After weeks coming up with next to nothing, certain this asteroid was empty, we'd found what the radar had promised us.

"Whoop, whoop!" Chelsea shouted, as she and Vivianna moved forward to hew the large chunk into smaller, finer pieces.

It was a breath of fresh air, this discovery. For months, all of Gragon 6 was lagging in its products. It seemed like all of a sudden the asteroids had stopped producing the ore. The belt around Gravion was an oddity enough in the cosmosphere—asteroids don't usually continuously produce ore. Everywhere else, once it was mined, it was gone. But not here.

Generations of miners lived, breathed, and bred on Gragon 6. Tradition hit hard in our homes, and it was with pride if one could say their family went back at least five generations. Newcomers were hard sought out, but also slowly welcomed into the community. It wasn't until they were two generations deep they'd be considered acquaintances, and not until four they were considered true Gragians.

I smiled as the excitement spread through the rest of the crew. This was huge for us. The first all-female crew in decades, we had a lot riding on our shoulders. Women were miners all the time, but some prejudices and ancient practices stood true in the colonies. Most women were kept in the home to raise the children, while the men went out to mine.

But this crew? These seven women that I oversaw, plus myself? We all came from families with only daughters. And when that fact came into play, we worked hard until we were put together as the only all-female running crew.

There was a lot to be proud of. As I glanced at each of the seven women at their post, I couldn't help but feel a swell of honour. We were smart, capable, and strong. Allison was the best driller of our generation. Other crews sought her out, but she refused to leave her twin's side. Katie and I had worked together as hurriers in another crew, and when I was finally promoted to foreman and could pick my own team, I snatched her right up. And Allison came with her.

Chelsea was a skilled breaker. She had a finesse in breaking out even the microbes of rock stuck to the alvionite, and it net us some of the cleanest product. The big boss was always pleased when he saw Chelsea's name attached to a shipment.

No shaft was safer under Gabby's hands. One of the fastest and best timbers I'd ever worked with, put her together with Delphine, the smartest engineer this side of Gravion, and I wouldn't sweat panning in the deepest of pits.

Vivianna came from one of the oldest families on Gragon 6, and Chunhua was one of the best first aids I'd seen in years. I was damn proud of my crew, and this newest vein of discovery would finally give us the credit we were long overdue. No more would we need to work harder to prove ourselves to the co-ed or all male crews.

"What's the plan? Should I cut more out?" Allison asked, as Chelsea and Vivianna moved a large chunk into one of the

carts. Together they started to chip away at the rock with their lasers, clearing it off of the precious ore.

I glanced at my watch. Our shift was over in thirty minutes. But if we left the vein open, another crew could sweep in and take the credit. The chunk we had already was quite large—probably the equivalent of our last five hauls. But as I peered into the cut rock over Allison's shoulder, there was no denying the shine of more waiting underneath.

"What do we think about overtime today, ladies?" I asked.

"For a score this big? Absolutely," Chelsea grinned.

I looked over at Gabby. "How's the holding? Do we have more time?"

Gabby tapped on the screen of the tablet in her hands. She then looked up at the red lines wavering along the seams of the cave and nodded her head. "Yup. At least four more hours before it starts to get overloaded."

Allison laughed as she flipped her face shield back down. "Four hours? Give me one, tops, and we'll have this baby emptied out."

The time went by quickly as we worked seamlessly. Well-oiled cogs in an old-fashioned clock, Allison dug deeper into the vein. Chelsea extracted it, and then she and Vivianna would clean it. Once clean, Katie would bring it to the surface and mark it with our code so nobody else could try to claim it as their own. Codes were not interchangeable. To try to tamper with someone else's score was one of Gragon's highest *offenses. We may have had to work harder to prove ourselves, but there was little doubt once our code was on something that they could try to take the achievement away.*

True to her word, just over an hour later the vein was empty. A few small pieces lay deep inside, too far for Chelsea to reach, and too delicate to carve out more with the laser drill.

"Let's pack up," I instructed. Allison let out a loud exhale, lifting her mask up and reclining back in the chair. Sweat beaded on her forehead, but her grin hadn't left her face. "We can check in next shift and see if we can get these pieces out with the hover, if they're still here."

"You know Jakeman's crew is going to scope it out once he sees how much we were able to get here," Chunhua muttered. She shifted the first aid bag over one shoulder and tossed her long, dark braid over the other.

"And he was the one who scoffed at the idea of checking such a small asteroid!" Gabby snickered.

I smirked. Evan Jakeman was about to eat his words, that was for sure. "Delphine, you run up this last bit while we finish. We'll meet you up there."

"You got it, boss!"

As Delphine disappeared up the tunnel with the cart, whistling a well-known Gragon 6 tune, the rest of us started to pack up. Spirits high, Katie started to hum the same tune, and everyone joined in. Allison carefully began to dismantle the drill and pack it away, her twin helping.

A light rumble sounded through the cavern. Immediately, I turned to Gabby, who started to tap away on her screen. The others froze, the music dying on their lips. Chunhua gripped her medical bag, and we held our breath, waiting. There hadn't been a cave collapse in over a year, which, unfortunately, was quite a long stretch. It was proud work, mining in the Gragon colonies, but it was dangerous.

"Everything is stable," Gabby said slowly, unease in her voice. Her hazel eyes went wide, and her head snapped up, gaze zeroing in on me. "I'm reading that someone has landed on the asteroid."

Frowning, I pulled out my comm. A tinier version of Gabby's tablet, I scrolled through my messages. "Maybe Vizal's checking in since we stayed overtime... though I don't see any messages from hi—"

A scream erupted from up the tunnel. It echoed as Delphine's footsteps slapped down the rock back towards us, followed by what sounded like a blaster's fire.

My head snapped back to Allison. "Quick, get the drill back together!"

Metal scraped together as Allison fumbled to put the machine back together. But even with Katie's help, it was too late. There wasn't enough time.

Delphine ran around the corner, tears streaming down her face. Her left leg limped behind her and her eyes were wide as they landed on me.

"Lisa, it's—"

A series of chirps flitted through the air, and a chill ran up my spine. I'd never seen them before, but everyone knew about the Skulchers. All humans were educated on them from a young age, regardless of where they lived in the galaxy.

Chunhua rushed forward as Delphine fell to the ground, screaming as the hot laser from the blaster hit her in the back. Blood started to seep onto the ground. The smell of singed skin wafted through the air, mixing with the smell of rock and ore—of home.

"Delphine!" Chunhua cried. "Stay still, stay with me."

I took a step forward to help, but froze as they came around the corner. Each carried a long, silver blaster in their large, three-fingered hands. Long grey faces with double-lidded eyes, and beak-like mouths, the Skulchers were some of the well-known faces in the galaxy. Public enemy number one for most species, especially humans. Their expertise was trafficking in goods, and people were their specialty.

Chunhua stood as the Skulchers approached, Delphine's lifeless body at her feet. She whipped out her standard issue knife and swiped it at the nearest alien. He was caught off guard, the blade ripping into his skin, and dark, green blood oozed over its silver suit.

He chirped something at Chunhua, his beady black eyes narrowing. Before anyone could blink, his hands reached out and the deafening snap of Chunhua's neck reverberated through the cave. My footsteps stuttered and halted, and one of the girls behind me let out a harrowing sob.

The Skulcher chirped something at us and raised his blaster in warning. The three behind him held theirs up as well. There was no need for a translation. We were going with them, or we'd end up dead like the other two.

"Are you fucking serious?" Allison shouted behind me. Three of the Skulchers entered the cave and surrounded us, rounding us up like cattle. Allison whipped out her own blade and turned around to face one of the them.

"Allison, stand down," I commanded. My hands were shaking, but my voice was firm. The snap of Chunhua's neck still echoed in my mind, and the smell of Delphine's flesh was fresh in the air. I would not let any more of my crew be killed.

Allison's knife clattered to the floor. Something beeped on one of the Skulchers' comms, and they started to push us out of the cavern. Katie sobbed as she stepped over the bodies, and my breath hitched at the sight of Chunhua's lolling neck. At the blood pooled underneath Delphine.

I had failed them.

"Lisa."

I jerk awake, my heart beating wildly. The memory turned nightmare recedes back into the depths of my mind, where it would wait until I slept again. Every time I close my eyes, that day replays in my head. The snap of Chunhua's neck would haunt me at every turn.

Slowly, my eyes focus on Katie and the ship around us. Outlined by the faint light of the ship and the bright snow from outside, her blond brows furrow as she searches my face. "You were whimpering in your sleep again."

I sit up slowly, rubbing the sands of sleep out of my eyes. "Sorry," I murmur.

"Nothing to be sorry about," Katie whispers sadly. She glances over her shoulder to the hallway. "Melanie is still asleep."

The last five days come flooding back as I gather our surroundings. We were kidnapped by trafficking aliens, managed to escape them, but crashed here. More than half of our group has been separated from us, and Evie has gone out for help. My heartbeat starts to calm as I take in the bridge. Snow has piled on the shuttle's windshield overnight. It blocks some of the sunlight that tries to pour into the room. The light is comforting, despite that it comes from a foreign sun. Despite that we're deserted on an uncharted planet, with no way to communicate for help. Despite that most of my Gragian crew is missing.

"Let her sleep," I say as I get to my feet. "Gives us a break from her negativity."

"I'm sure she's just scared," Katie says quietly. Maybe, but I doubted it. There was something about her attitude that just screams privilege, and given she was taken from Lagusta, it fits.

"Any word from Evie?" I ask. Katie shakes her head, and I sigh. My skin itches underneath the familiar black miner's suit. The rest of my girls are out there. I failed two of them in the mines, and it haunts me every day. I glance sideways at Katie and take a deep breath. "OK. Let's see what else we can repair in here, and hope she contacts soon."

Katie gets to work, tapping and flicking switches on the shuttle's dashboard. A project will keep her busy and her mind off finding Allison. If it weren't for her, I'd have gone out to find the others. Maybe the two of us out there would have been better than one, but I think Katie would have slowed me down. It would have been ideal to leave her here in the shelter, but I know she'd be uncomfortable without me being present. Katie is a whiz when it comes to astronavigation, and she is a good tinkerer, but a soft-hearted soul. She worries about things endlessly, sometimes to perfection, and if there was something she couldn't fix? Like finding her sisters and the others? It would destroy her.

The better option was to let Evie go. She has people to find, too. I can trust her to be earnest in her search. But as I turn back to look out the windshield, the breeze fluttering a chunk of snow off the glass, I wish it were me out there. Because this time, I knew I wouldn't fail them.

Katie sighs. "She's going the wrong way."

"What?" I ask, head snapping up. I'm trying to see if I can fix another one of the mobile comms, see if I can get it to work at a longer range. Maybe we can get contact with the cargo hold, despite the bridge telling us otherwise.

"Evie," Katie says. She gestures at the screen in front of her. "She's here, but the cargo hold signal is coming from this way."

As though speaking her name has summoned her, there's a crack of static. "Lisa? Come in, Lisa."

Evie's voice, gravelly through the comm's speaker, fills the bridge. My heart skips a beat as I jump up and stand by Katie's side. "Evie! Where the hell are you? What happened, are you ok?"

"I'm fine. I walked all day, was almost attacked by a wolf and a leope, and found shelter for the night."

Relief floods through me. At least she survived and found shelter. Maybe this would work out after all. Maybe she is more of a survivalist than I first thought...

Leope? Did she say leope? "A leope? What the hell is that?" I ask.

"Must be one of the thousands of species I scanned on the way in," Katie murmured. "Let me see if I can catalog it..."

"It's like a leopard—which is a big cat on Terra," Evie says. Interesting, though there are no cats on Gragon 6 so I'm not sure what to picture. "But that's not important, I—"

"You're going in the wrong direction," Melanie suddenly drawls through the system, her hand on the speaker. She joined us about an hour ago. There's only so many places to sulk in the ship.

"You've gone west instead of east," Katie says softly, always trying to make sure nobody's upset. She's the peacemaker, which I'm thankful for since we're stuck here with Melanie and my patience is waning with her. "But you made quite a distance. It's impressive."

It is, I'll give her that. But she's wasted time. I eye the screen, measuring the distance in my head from the solid blue light of the bridge, to the red blinking one of Evie's location.

"The compass doesn't work!" Evie's voice cracks over the comm. "Everything out here is snow and mountain. It all looks the same."

"It's ok," I say quickly, needing her to calm down. There is no time to waste on hysterics. "We can get you back on the right path. Are you out trekking right now?"

"No, I'm not," Evie says. My heart plummets, but I inhale slowly. It's ok. She's likely just woken up. *If we can get her back here, I'm going to take her place. Broken compass or not, I know I can find the others faster. Katie will just have to deal with some separation anxiety for a few days.* "But I have good news. I think I've found some—*oh no*—"

There's no mistaking the panic that seeps into Evie's voice. It's palpable even through the shoddy comm. Katie glances up at me, worry in her eyes, and even Melanie shifts uncomfortably.

"Evie? Evie, what's wrong?" I ask.

But Evie never answers. There's static a few times, and then the line goes silent. We collectively hold our breaths, watching as her signal continues to blink.

The light stays on, thankfully. It doesn't disappear, but Evie's voice doesn't come back through the comm again. Whatever happened has taken priority. We'll just have to keep an eye on her signal and pray it doesn't go out.

Slowly, I sigh and let out my held breath. I turn to the others and shrug my shoulders. "Guess we get back to work here."

"Doing what?" Melanie snarks.

It's only been one day since Evie left, and already I want to wring Melanie's neck. I don't know how she dealt with this Pessimistic Penny for days on end, crammed in the same cell on the Skulchers' ship.

"Doing whatever we can to keep busy and send a signal for help."

LISA

DAY 4

The wind is brisk. My miner's suit is well suited for most climates. Designed from a synthetic fabric created by the Gragon people specifically for mining, it's meant to keep me warm in the cold and cool in the heat. It was smart for Evie to swap suits with Katie. She would have frozen otherwise.

The cold still bites at my exposed cheeks as I climb up onto the roof of the shuttle. Conserving the ship's energy is crucial. Forget trying to get a signal out for rescue, it's a matter of survival. The food is rationed, and we have a small cache of fresh water. Neither is dependent on the ship's energy, but our heat is. We've kept it low, just warming it enough to be comfortable. If it goes, we'll need to find another source for heat.

As I climb onto the top of the ship, I take in my surroundings. Evie was right. It's nothing but endless rocky terrain and snow. We're walled in on all sides by mountains and cliffs, and I see little in the way of trees for firewood. Heat will be a dream of the past if there's nothing to build a fire with and the ship's energy fails.

The snow shimmers in the sunlight as I trudge through it on the roof, careful of where I'm stepping. We're lucky the bridge didn't flip or crash onto its side on impact. It's positioned upward, though it leans a bit to the right. I don't think about what kind of condition the cargo hold is in, or how it would have landed. Evie steered us down to the ground, but they had an unexpected free fall. My stomach plummets at the memory.

A shiver races through me, and I try to push out the other thoughts that accompany it—the dark ones on whether they've survived. *They're fine*, the stubborn optimism in me whispers. My girls are tough. I know they are. As mean as it sounds, I have the weakest Gragian with me here. Katie is smart—no doubt about that—but she doesn't handle dangerous situations well. We had one close call with a cave-in about a year ago, and though nobody got hurt, there was always a level of worry in her eye on the job ever since. I can't imagine the anxiety coursing through her veins now, desperate to find her twin, but I imagine it's parallel to the determination I have about finding the others. It's priority number one.

According to the schematic and blueprints Katie pulled from the ship, there should be three solar panels somewhere to my right. I'm careful not to trip over any of the metal fixings and grips that jut up through the snow or lay hidden underneath. The last thing I need is to break something, either on the ship or my own bones, and put us in an even direr situation.

With my foot, I start to push the snow out of the way as I get to the spot. Once the bulk of it is cleared, I kneel down and start to brush the rest of it out of the way with my gloved hands.

The sunlight is bright as it glints off the glass panels. The shine nearly blinds me as the brush of my gloves reveal the energy banks. To my dismay, once all three are clear it looks like only one is functional.

"Katie was right," I murmur to myself as I stare down at them. She worried only one was working based on the readings she got from the ship. Two have large cracks on the surface, and the power indicators next to them are dead. But the third one's light flickers orange once all the snow is cleared and the sunlight hits it in full force. It's charging.

"One is better than none, I suppose," I continue aloud with a sigh.

I climb back down and head toward the door into the ship. The blue light around the open doorway is solid, the shield nearly invisible but obvious to those who know what to look for. It wavers for a moment, a flicker of energy, but then returns to solid. This flimsy Skulcher technology is what keeps us safe at night and from freezing to death.

As I bang my gloves together to clear off the sticky snow, Katie pops her head out of the bridge and comes to stand just on the other side of the door. I'm still not used to seeing her in Evie's blue jumpsuit instead of her black miner's gear.

"I just got off the comm with Evie."

My brow arches as I continue to shake the snow off my gloves. "And? Is she on her way?"

"She's headed north off track a bit, but I'm sure she'll find her way," Katie answers. A groan escapes me before I can stop it. *Shit.* "She's trying her best, Lisa."

I sigh. My eyes close and I take a deep breath. *It's only been two days since she's left. Give it more time.* Something snaps in the distance, and Chunhua's lolling head flashes in my mind. My eyes snap open, desperate to find the danger. But it's only Melanie opening the already emptied closet, searching for something.

The glum woman mutters something before the closet snaps shut again, and she sulks off into the single sleeping quarters where she's been holed up most of the time.

"I know," I say once the door closes behind Melanie. Gloves cleared off, I step through the force-field into the ship. I tap on the panel next to the wall and the shield turns from blue to red, indicating it's locked. It'll burn anything that dares try to step through it. "I just want to find the others."

"I do too," Katie says, that soft tone in her voice again. "I'm trying my best to see if we can communicate with the cargo hold. It would be odd for there to be no comm system within the ship, but maybe when it ripped apart it became damaged."

"I'm sure they're fine. Allison is tough, and Vivianna is resourceful. There's also that fighter-woman with them who knows about the Skulchers more than we do. I'm sure she's working on repairs on their end, too. I worry about Gabby's leg—"

"They'll take care of her," Katie echoes. "And from the trajectory of the signal, before we lost it, Briley is heading towards them. The fighter pod is meant to eject, it was probably the best equipped."

A quiet sense of remorse falls between us. Maybe it's part grief. Whatever it is, it's too quiet, and the vacuum of silence becomes too much.

"Did Evie say anything else?" I ask. The cargo hold was nothing but a metal box. Like a tin can under a giant's foot, it's probably nothing but rubble now. I need to change the subject from the missing women I'm responsible for and their uncertainty before the guilt consumes me.

Katie nods, and there's an excited shine in her eyes. "Yes! She ran into a local. Her translator broke, so they didn't get to exchange much information, but she says he's intelligent. And didn't seem hostile. But that was her first night, and she hasn't seen him since. She's been traveling with a wolf though…"

JUK

DAY 5

Anticipation buzzes through my fur as I complete my shift. My Seeker is clear, scanning the horizon as I bound forward on four paws.

Run to the south valley. There, you will find a strange, sleek rock. From the distance, it may appear small, but I believe it to be bigger—the size of a small cave.

My alpha's words ring through my head as I run ahead as fast as my paws will carry me. The task from my alpha is clear—investigate the fallen rock from four days ago.

I recall the image of the dark streak in the sky falling forward from the entrance of the den. Our alpha had already left on his search of Jenneka—I roll my eyes thinking about her and her antics—and it was my duty to keep the pack safe. Kalpa was first to spot it, waiting anxiously at the top of the ridge for sight of his runaway sister.

We thought nothing of it, as stars mean nothing to Snowscapes. It was an omen for the Stygians. Vekao was warning them of their foolishness, urging them to straighten their ways before she struck them down. Of course, the Stygians have been worshiping the stars since the creation. I would never call Vekao foolish for thinking she could change their minds now, but I do wonder what the omen means for them. What have they done to cause such a smite.

It is not your duty to question Vekao and her ways, my Seeker tells me. Despite it being a sign for the Stygians, I ordered the pack to stay inside the rest of that day. A storm approached at any rate, and by next morning, the dark streak had dissipated. Brex was curious about it, but I quashed his curiosities, and we did not bring it up again to the pack. Everyone had forgotten about it—until now.

I did not get a good look at the alpha's mate when they arrived. Jenneka said he was coming back with an *oddity*, something I would never use to describe an alpha's mate. Every mating is worthy of celebration, but an *alpha's* mating is best for the pack. It will bring strength to the Snowscapes. Solidity and prosperity. It is something that, for all we knew, is lacking in the other two packs. But, from the brief glimpse I got of the small female in the alpha's arms, she has no Seeker. No fluff of tails either. *An oddity indeed*.

My nose wrinkles at the thought of the Ashen and Stygian packs. We have little way of intel into either enemy's territory. Vekao would give a sign if either alpha had mated. The Stygians' den is too far from ours to get any sort of reading. They keep to their territory, as we do ours, which, oddly given their nature, makes them the better neighbours of our two rival packs.

The Ashen alpha is new. That is one thing a whisper on the wind told the patrol last time they were out that way. Their previous Alpha had been usurped and a new one is in place. Unless the new Alpha was already mated when he won the challenge...

I shake my head. Impossible. Vekao would tell us.

My paws are light on the snow, despite the enormity of my body. As the largest of my pack, my legs are strong. The southern valley is a half-day away at a good pace. The sun is already over the half-mark for the day, and the moons will be bright by the time I get there. But the sky looks clear, void of any new storms heading this way. I will investigate what I can, if anything, in the dark, before doing more in the daylight.

As the sky turns dark and Vekao's bright presence brightens the snow, I spot it. Axyll was not kidding in his description of it.

From afar, it looks like every other rock. It juts out from the ground, and snow coats most of it. But its scent is what hits me first. Metallic and tangy. Even from high up in the valley, the smell carries on the wind. It is foreign to our territory—to our world—and does not belong here. *I wonder if all fallen stars smell the same*.

As I climb down the valley's steep cliffs, the rock grows in size, just as Axyll predicted. By the time I reach it, it stands over me like a cave covered in snow. Its color is black, as dark as the night sky. Vekao's rays of moonlight bounce off the sides that are exposed.

I approach it with caution. The smell is stronger here and burns my nostrils. My Seeker starts to shine though, and my hearts thump loudly in my chest. This is a different feeling than my usual intuition. It is not telling me of what will happen, or what is to come. There is no danger here, but there is *something*. Something of such importance that it blinds me for a moment and I must look away.

Once it has calmed down, I start to sniff where the walls meet the snow. Most of it is buried under the white fluff. As I scan what I presume is the front of it, I notice what looks like a crack near the top. But the wall there is clear. It's as clear as a frozen pond. All it reveals is darkness on the other side, and I stare at it in wonder. It makes no sense to me why a star would have a frozen pond on its front.

And then, suddenly, something shifts from within the cave. A piece of snow falls from the frozen pond affixed to its front, and I see a quick glimpse of something inside. A pale, Seekerless face shines in Vekao's moonlight. A female. My Seeker shines so brightly I blink to clear my head, and when I open my eyes again, she is gone. There is only darkness on the other side of the frozen pond.

Perhaps I imagined it, I think to myself, but by the hammering of my hearts and the flip of my stomach, I know it is not true. My fur stands on end, and I turn my head to look up at Vekao, begging her for guidance.

It will be easier to discern what I am looking at—what I saw—during the light of day. I will return to the cave in the morning, under the sun's bright rays, and then I will uncover the mystery of this strange, fallen star.

I sleep at a distance from the sleek cave. It's in my sight, a black blip in the bright snow. The unfamiliar smells and that flash of a pale face through the pond-wall cause a restless slumber. I wake long before dawn. By the time the sun is dominant and Vekao has faded into the bright blue of the sky, I've eaten a small drackyr poached from a nearby nesting ground and head back to the cave with a full belly.

The sun is bright this day. It reflects off the snow, the sparkle of the cold powder shimmering under its rays. A breeze rustles my fur. My tracks from earlier this morning have been disturbed by the wind, half-covered with the shifting snow.

I approach the cave from the west. The metallic stench grows stronger the closer I get. It is an odd, unpleasant scent that I have little to compare to. Axyll's mate had traces of it still on her when they arrived at the den, but I did not get a good glimpse of her before she was whisked off to Nyfer.

As I slink closer to the looming black shape, many thoughts and emotions fly at me. There is happiness for my cousin and my best friend, my alpha, for finding his mate. But there is a wariness too. His mate is not a Celetan. From the brief glimpse I did get of her, she is small and fragile. Her forehead runs smooth, no scar of a ripped-out Seeker or birth deformity, and she had no underlying scent of a celestial form. Never has there been a Celetan with such features.

I stare up at the smooth walls of the cave—the fallen star—and lift my nose. Taking a deep whiff, I filter through the different scents coming at me. The metallic is the strongest. It is everywhere, and I categorize it in my mind as part of the cave itself. The smell permeates from the black walls, and must have to do with their composition. Beneath that, there are various other scents. Rock, earth, blood, sweat. But nowhere do I detect the scent I am trying to find, the one that has my hearts beating hard in my chest with fear and anger: the scent of the Stygians.

The dark pack from the north are our enemies. I did not scent them on the cave yesterday either, but now, in the light of day, I need to be sure. They're an affront to nature, their minds addled and evil as they choose to worship the stars instead of Vekao. Even the Ashen pack, who worship Jaci, Vekao's smaller ward, are better than the Stygians. They, too, are our enemy, but they are reasonable. They can be reasoned *with*. The Stygians are nothing but monsters.

I am hesitant as I start to circle to the other side of the cave. Cautious optimism tries to calm my nerves, as nowhere do I catch the filthy stench of a Stygian. *Perhaps Axyll is right: this fallen star is a warning to the Stygians, not a threat to the Snowscapes. This is not of their doing—this will be their undoing.*

I often stare up at the stars. They twinkle, bright and distant, far inferior to Vekao and Jaci. There *is* a beauty to them I dare not admit aloud, but they are nothing special. Nothing to worship in a snub to Vekao. There is something calming about them. And yet, as I slowly circle this one now, I never imagined this as their appearance. Dark like the night sky, with smooth walls, there is no beauty to it up close. Aside from the reflection of the sun's rays, it does not shine. There is the strangeness of the see-through wall, like ice on a clear pond, and as I inspect closer, I see orange flecks here and there amongst the black. The orange flecks permeate the metallic burning stench the strongest.

There is a light. My Seeker guides me round the corner of the cave and a new scent hits me. It is similar to the scent of a flame, but lighter. It is almost unnoticeable next to the overwhelming metallic that covers everything. As I round the corner, I see it. A wavering red light outlines the entrance to the cave.

My pulse quickens again as I stare into the cave. There is a nearly invisible red wall blocking the entrance. It stretches out from the red light surrounding the entrance. I do not understand it, but I do not trust it. My Seeker warns me not to cross it.

The inside of the cave is dark through the red veil. Beyond its burning scent, my nose picks up different smells. There is more sweat and blood, and metallic is the strongest of all again. But there is also a sweetness I cannot describe. It is faint, wafting from further inside the cave. There is also the concealed smell of feces and urine rotting from the left.

My ear twitches. Soft voices speak inside the darkness. They are female, their words foreign to me. I think back to the face I saw the night before, the brief glimpse of a being inside the cave. An involuntary, soft whine escapes me. I want to see these females up close, see if they reek of the Stygians. I want to know how many there are, and if they are Seekerless like Axyll's mate. But the red glow across the entrance is impassable.

I decide, then, that the best course of action is to round back to where the clear wall is. The one that I can see through and see the females. Perhaps then I can get their attention. *Would it be better if you were in your ancestral form?* my mind wonders. Then I could call out to the females from this side of the red warning.

I turn away from the red glow and start to round the cave, still unsure of which idea is best. My alpha commanded for me to come and see what was hidden in the cave. I know it is females, but I need to see them. I need to know how many before heading back with my report. Is his mate aware of the females here? Was she in this fallen star with them? Axyll did not know what the stare contained, which means he must have met her elsewhere, away from this shiny cave.

Something cold and hard suddenly hits my fur. I do not stumble, for my strong legs hold me in place, but I am bewildered.

"Oooo aaayyy!"

I look up as another snowball pelts into me. This one hits me in the face, on my right side as I turn out of the way too slowly. The cold, compact snow does not hurt as it hits my jaw, but it is an annoyance. Snow falls into my eye, and sticks to my fur as I shake my face.

When my vision has cleared, I look up at the source of the assault. My Seeker is blinded by the reflection of the sun on the cave—or so I tell myself—as the outline of a petite female is silhouetted against the sun. All I make out is black hair blowing in the lazy breeze and dark, strong eyes glaring down at me. And the lack of a Seeker.

"Eeet ooout oooof eeere!" she shouts again, as her hands compact the snow into another ball. I dodge this one easily, but the message is clear. She is not afraid, but protective of those inside the cave. She does not understand that I mean them no harm. The female is quick to throw another snowball at me, and I retreat further back.

With one last look at the female atop the cave, I push off with my paws and race back to the den. The sun is past the midday mark, and Vekao looms in the distance. By the time I reach the den, the sun will have set and it will be nightfall.

I push as fast as my legs will take me. My paws barely touch the snow before they are off again, bounding me forward as my mind reels at the discovery. There are more females like Axyll's strange mate. And, as far as I can tell, there is no scent of Stygian on them.

By the time I reach the den, my legs are aching. Vekao is bright and full in the sky. She looms over the mountains and dwarfs Jaci. The snow is glittering in her reflection.

As I reach the bottom of the cliff, I spot the familiar glow of a fire's flame on the plateau. *The Celestial Moon Bonfire*, my mind reminds me. They are celebrating on the plateau in front of the den. The entire pack will be out there and present for my announcement.

At the bottom of the cliff, I shift as fast as possible. It is nearly seamless, my bones snapping all at once, and shifting back into place of my ancestral form. My white fur recedes into my body, replaced with thick skin that keeps my bones and innards warm. I am panting by the time it is done. My arms shake as I sweep my hair up into a knot at the top of my head with a piece of scrap leather that I keep on me at all times.

Just looking at the holdings scaling up the cliff to the den makes me feel tired. I have not eaten anything since this morning and have pushed myself all afternoon to get home. But my alpha must learn of this discovery right away. He will want to know there are more females who, in my opinion, may be in distress. The smell of feces and urine that wafted out of the cave replays in my memory, as well as the underlying scent of blood.

My arms still shaking, I climb up the holdings as fast as possible. As I pull myself over the cliff's edge, my fingers threaten to slip on the icy surface, but I grunt through it.

I hesitate for only a moment as I stand, my heart dropping into the pit of my stomach as I take in the scene before me. My alpha is in the middle of his bonding ceremony. To be united under a full Vekao is one of the greatest blessings possible. And here I am about to interrupt it.

Axyll does not notice me at first, as he glares over at his uncle, Joval. Perhaps I am not the first to interrupt the ceremony then. Brex lets out a warning growl, and Joval huffs in response.

The alpha then turns his attention to me as I make quick strides over to him. His mate is small and meek beside him. She is the same size as an adolescent, only a few fingers taller than Hexa. Her small round face looks at me curiously, and my stomach twists at her lack of a Seeker. I do not understand Axyll's choice in her, but I know his Seeker has guided him. Has decided they are to be mates. It is Vekao's wish, and I will not question or stop it. Her will is absolute, especially on a day such as this when she is full in the sky.

"Juk," my alpha says. There is curiosity in his blue eyes.

"I have been to the fallen star," I say. My hearts thump wildly, my lungs still trying to catch a breath. Nyfer listens carefully next to me. "There are no Stygians, no trace of them. But there are females—females like her. And they need our help."

JUK

DAY 7

"I can't believe there are more females," Brex says. His tails wag with excitement as he packs another bundle of furs into the sled. All morning, we have been hastily putting together supplies to rescue the other women. Axyll's mate, Ee-vee, confirmed that her people are in distress. It makes sense why she was so desperate to get back to the fallen-star-cave.

Brex looks up at me with shining eyes. He runs a hand through his close-cropped hair, the front fringe flopping into his eyes as he grins sheepishly at me. "Maybe there will be a mate for me there."

I grunt in response. My breath puffs before me, but it is quite warm this day. The sun shines down, having just risen from its slumber. Axyll wants to reach the cave and bring the females back to the den before nightfall. As a result, Brex and I have been up since before dawn to assemble the sled, and start the preparation of supplies.

Baz scoffs as he comes up from behind me. "You want a mate with no Seeker?"

Brex shrugs. "The alpha's mate is not so terrible to look at, is she? She seems kind enough. That is what is important to me. Vekao has presented us with this gift for a reason. If she sees one of them fit enough to mate the alpha, then who is to say that there could not be one for me? For a few of us?"

Baz rolls his eyes and shoves another roll of furs at Brex. "Always with your head in the clouds, dreaming of nonsense," he murmurs as he turns to go shift around the corner. The alpha's mate does not like the sight of our shifting, and he has requested we do it outside of both her eyesight and earshot.

One of many changes, perhaps, with this new alpha-mate, I wonder as I watch Baz disappear. What else will change with the arrival of more of her kind? Are we to cater to each of them as they disrupt the pack?

My Seeker flashes. It's a vision of the female atop the cave. Her dark eyes burn into mine, yet the rest of her features are silhouetted against the sun. Her aim is impeccable as the snowball hits my muzzle. It does not hurt, but I know her arm is strong. The memory is brief, disappearing as fast as it came.

I shake my head, clearing my mind's eye. *My Seeker was blinded by the sun—nothing more*, I lie to myself. If Brex knew of what my Seeker was telling me, of what I refuse to admit until I see her up close, then his delusions would overflow, and his tails would wag so fast they would break right off.

Axyll soon appears at the top of the plateau, giving the signal for me to go shift. His small mate appears beside him. Her pale face is determined, peeking out from the furs wrapped around her. It is the face of a leader determined to find her people. Perhaps she is a good mate for my alpha after all. But then I think again of the silhouetted one, the fearlessness in her voice and the force behind her throw as she warned me to stay away from the cave. Do they follow more than one leader, these people? Is the alpha's mate actually a beta?

As the alpha and his mate make their descent down the cliff's holdings, I walk around the corner to shift out of sight. Kalpa and Amble come round the corner in their celestial forms. They both nod their heads to me in passing. I hear the last few snaps of Baz's bones as he completes his transformation, and I stop a few paces away from him.

I untie the scrap of leather from around my hair. The yellow strands fall to my shoulders, trailing over the tops of them as I tightly bind the wrap around my ankle. Once the scrap is secured, tied as tight as possible so it remains there once I have shifted, I get down on all fours. I spot Brex rounding the corner to come shift before my vision blurs and the transformation begins.

My limbs are the first to snap, wrists breaking as they bend to their new formation. My arms and legs elongate, as my fingers become stout and my nails thicker and longer. Fur sprouts all over my body in a rippling wave as my cheek bones crack and my snout emerges, molded out from my nose. My gums sting as my teeth elongate, and my fangs poke out from my lips.

The whole ordeal takes less than a minute. My heartsbeat ramps up during the process but calms as I stand on all four legs. My tails swish, testing the wind, feeling the air for any sign of an impending storm. My intuition tells me it will be clear. Good.

Axyll is the last to shift. I stand guard by the sled, side-eying his mate as we wait. She is tucked in next to all the furs. The fire of determination still burns in her small eyes, and she glances at me for a moment before turning her attention to the alpha. He comes back around the bend quickly, already in his celestial form. It is a gift to the alpha, to be able to shift so quickly. Relief splashes across his mate's face quickly, and he readies himself at the pulley for the sled.

With a subtle nod, we are off.

I charge at the front of the pack. I will guide them to the fallen star, to the black shiny cave. Brex and Baz flank the alpha, while Kalpa and Amble take the rear. The omega starts off beside Amble on the right, before running out into the outer ring of our formation. He scouts it from the back to the front, and then charges off ahead of me to scout for danger. His small form is nothing but a blur when he is beside me, and then he is out of sight, blended in with the snow.

The trek is slower with the group than it was for me yesterday. With the alpha pulling the sled, we do not run at top speed. Clouds blot out the sun, but by the time I spot the shiny cave I am sure it is just past midday. I let out a howl, notifying the rest of our arrival, and pick up the pace. There is a rumble of thunder in the distance, but it is not heading our way. Our mission will not be interrupted by a storm, of this I am certain.

The cave is buried in snow. Mounds of the cold white fluff are piled against its sides. Its clear wall is barely visible, and if not for the black speck peeking out on top, it could easily be mistaken for a boulder. The sun shines through the clouds at this moment, reflecting off the clear wall exposed at the top. It reminds me of my shining Seeker from yesterday, and something in my stomach flips.

Axyll pulls up beside me. Before he even stops, his mate rips off the furs around her and jumps into the snow. It nearly swallows her up to her hips. The alpha yips a quick command at us to stay with the sled while the two of them move forward.

They disappear around to the back of the cave. Axyll's bones snap as he shifts back into his ancestral form, and Brex shoots me a querying look. He tilts his head to the side, and lets out a small huff.

Should we follow?

I start to shake my head but then pause as I remember the red glow from the cave's entrance. I forgot to warn the alpha about it. His mate may know what it means, but he does not. I listen to my intuition, wondering if perhaps this is a Stygian trap after all. It senses no danger, but I always err on the side of caution. I nod to Brex, and lead the way.

As I round the corner to the entrance, I pause. The red glow is no longer there. Instead, it has been replaced with a blue one. The colour is soft and inviting, the same colouring as many of the Snowscape Celetans. I hesitate, wary of its change. It could be a trap, a falsity luring us into the cave. I then see that my alpha has crossed through the wall and stands in the cave. His back is to us, his tails twitching momentarily as he stands next to his mate.

An unfamiliar female voice suddenly speaks, and every strand of my fur goes on edge. It is not out of fear, but a jittery apprehension. My Seeker blinds me momentarily as I try to peer around my alpha and his mate to look at the female. My hearts beat so wildly I worry they will seize and fail.

She stands in front of the alpha's mate and looks over her shoulder. Our eyes meet and a jolt of lightning fires through me. It strikes me to my core and my Seeker is blinded. My hearts beat faster as her dark eyes meet mine. I must shift to meet her.

Without hesitation, I bear down to shift. With the first crack of my bones, however, I notice the female flinches. It is a brief reaction, and she is quick to hide it, but the message is clear to me. The sounds of the process are disturbing to her. I do not want to make her uncomfortable. A surge of protectiveness courses through me as I finish shifting as fast as possible. The females in the cave continue to talk, and soon they are walking further inside, Axyll following.

"Go shift outside of earshot of the females," I instruct to the others once I am in my ancestral form. Brex nods and leads the others out of sight around the back of the cave. I will not have the sounds of their shifts disturb the dark-haired female that makes my pulse light with fire. I throw on a breechcloth, as my alpha wears one. His mate is shy around the naked form, and I assume these other females may be the same.

Without trepidation, I pass through the blue wall and into the cave. My knuckles scrape the top of the cave as I pull my hair up and out of my face. The cave is small and the metallic smell reeks everywhere. The scent of feces and urine wafts out from behind a wall.

The females talk excitedly in another part of the cave. There is a light-haired one who gestures towards the alpha, but I barely notice her. My eyes go to the petite dark-haired one. There is a frown on her face, but as her eyes flicker to me and meet mine, my breath stops. She is beautiful. Her skin is tawny, different from the pale colour of the other three. Her eyes are different too, beautiful in their angular shape and dark brown colour.

Axyll's mate is introducing them to one another. I stumble over his mate's name in my head, but remind myself to make it a habit to use her name and not just think of her as "the alpha's mate."

Ee-vee, I remind myself.

"*Leesa*," the female with the burning eyes says. It flows off her tongue eloquently, just as fluid as the rest of their strange language. It is a beautiful name that the alpha butchers, but I am determined not to.

"*Leesa*," I say with confidence the first time. Her eyes snap to me, surprised, and Ee-vee shoots me a smile. I miss the others' names, my eyes focused on Leesa. My pulse quickens every time she looks at me, and my tails twitch. The smooth plane on her forehead furrows together when she catches me looking at her, and I turn away. I do not want to scare her.

Suddenly, there is a screeching sound and a spear descends from the ceiling. A growl escapes my lips before I can stop it as I watch the spindly thing come out from the ceiling's rock.

It's thin, thinner than one of the bone sewing needles Hexa uses for her embroidery designs. On its end is a red, rounded bump. And it points directly at my alpha.

Ee-vee starts to gesture at the spear and then to Axyll. Words spill quickly from her mouth, excitement radiating off her. I don't understand what she is saying, but she keeps gesturing to the spear. She then says something to the lighter-haired one, and I search my intuition for if this situation is about to turn sour. My Seeker studies the spear, but cannot determine if it is a threat.

It is a spear—of course it is a threat, I think to myself. And it points right to my alpha.

"It will teach us their speech," Axyll whispers suddenly. His head whips back up to the spear, his gaze torn from his mate.

I bristle next to him and follow his eye to the thing. "How?"

Ee-vee nods with excitement again, and gestures towards the spear. She taps the side of her head. An unsettling chill runs through my body as the meaning dawns on me, and my alpha speaks. "It will put it into our head."

My tails twitch. I eye the spear again, desperate to know if it is harmful or not. But my intuition is silent, for once. I feel uncomfortable as I argue against my alpha. It goes against everything a Celetan is, and my stomach twists. "Absurd. It is a spear, Alpha. A weapon—not something of knowledge. How do we know they speak the truth? How do we know it is not a trap?"

I inhale deeply, trying again to catch any trace of Stygian scent. But there is nothing. Yet they point a spear at my alpha's head and claim it to hold knowledge. It is just as absurd as worshipping the stars.

The alpha is not concerned. He trusts his mate and her people. There is no trace of a Stygian trap inside this odd, metallic star, and my intuition tells me there is no danger. But it still worries me. I look at the spear, uncertain as my alpha tries to reassure me.

"I will go first, Alpha," I decide. I square my shoulders, standing as tall as possible. If this is a trap, these females would be unwise to try to take down a Celetan as big as me. "Once we determine it is safe, then you may face the language-spear. Until then, it is my duty to keep you safe. For the pack."

Axyll sighs next to me and relents. As he steps aside and I take his place, he explains to the females that I will go first. They understand his gestures, and the light-haired one nods at me to step into place.

The spear is just above my head. It looks harmless, like one of the thin bones of a drakyr's wing. They are good for picking meat out between my fangs, and I want to chuckle at the comparison. I could snap this spear with one hand. And yet...

Apprehension eats away inside me as Ee-vee adjusts my position. Her hands are small, tiny on my arms as she turns me, so the spear points to the side of my head. Now I cannot face it head on, and the uncertainty knotting in my stomach becomes worse. My hearts beat loudly, drumming inside my chest as clear as the Celestial Moon Bonfire's drums, but I keep my face calm. I will not show fear.

The light-haired one says something unintelligible in their language. There is a brief, hot sting to the side of my head, and suddenly everything goes black.

My head aches, as though someone has smashed a boulder over it. I let out a groan as its pangs are felt throughout my entire body. My limbs tremble everywhere, and there are soft voices somewhere above me.

"Slowly, Juk," Axyll says. I feel his hands slip under me, helping me to sit upright.

As my eyes slowly open, the first thing they lock onto is Leesa. Her dark eyes watch me carefully. She sits close to me on my right side, and her scent overpowers me. It is sweet and foreign, a mixture of minerals I am unfamiliar with and an underlying floral I cannot place. It is intoxicating, and it takes all my control not to lean over and breathe in a deep whiff. I want it to replace the air that I breathe. I want to bathe in it.

"How do you feel?" Axyll asks.

"Dizzy," I say. I feel my temple where the light spear was pointed. It is tender, but not painful. It stings like a light scratch, but the feeling fades quickly. I start to tell my alpha as such, when I pause and turn towards the females.

There are words in my head that I suddenly know. Another language mixed in there along with my native tongue, but I am too stunned to start the conversation. Too much in disbelief that this is real, that a spindly spear from inside a rock placed the knowledge there.

"Hi Juk," Ee-vee says in her fluid words. Fluid words I now understand. My tails swish and my hearts beat with excitement. It worked. "Can you understand me?"

"Yes, I can. It worked," I respond. I can't comprehend how I know the words that I speak now, only that I do. They come as naturally as my own language, and I can feel the excitement radiating off Axyll as I speak the new language.

Soon, my alpha and the others all take the language-spear. Each one collapses after it zaps into their head, but they are not out long.

But the new language is not the most surprising thing from the trip to the fallen star. There are other females—*Teerans* they call their people—scattered across the territories. Three groups it seems. One is in Snowscape territory, but her star on the map is no longer accurate. But the other eight are in Stygian territory.

"The *Stygians*," I explain through grit teeth when Ee-vee asks what it means, "are an abomination."

My alpha is more eloquent with his words, telling the females they are nothing more than a rival pack to the north. "They are never to be trusted."

I tune out the rest of his explanation as I try to calm my pulse as I look at the star on the map. One for sure is in Stygian territory. She is a lost cause, in my eyes. The Stygians will rip her apart, if they have not already. But the other seven... it is unclear. They are together as a group, the females explain, in another cave much like this one. Their star lies right on the border of Snowscape and Stygian territory.

The sullen one, a female with a sour face and long dark hair, argues with me about what is so wrong with the Stygians. They are Celetans too, but they are horrible. She does not understand that their faith in the stars is an abomination against Vekao and everything it *means* to be Celetan. There is no point in arguing with someone who cannot understand.

My alpha decides we should go find the woman who is already in Snowscape territory. But Leesa is firm in her words.

"No," she interrupts my alpha. I bristle at her rudeness, but it also sends a thrill through me. She is so strong. The Teerans claim to have no alpha, no leader, but Leesa possesses the qualities of one. Every time her eyes meet mine, there is something fierce in them. And it makes fire run through my veins.

"We go here first," she continues and points to the star on the territory line. "This is the top priority. The others can wait."

Axyll bristles as Leesa continues to argue, with both him and Ee-vee. I stay silent and watch. The females at this star are very important to her. Perhaps not all of these Teerans come from the same pack. And that will spell even more trouble than I first imagined.

LISA

The ride back to the Celetan's cave—den, they call it—is quiet. We've been traveling for an hour or two, wrapped in furs and bundled into the sled like Gravion peas in a pod. I keep my arm wrapped around Katie's shoulder and she leans on me. She lets out a quiet whimper now and then when the sled hits a rough patch, but otherwise the only sound is the wind whooshing by us and the wolves' paws hitting the snow. Melanie sits on the other side of Katie, squished against the side of the sled.

The decision is not the one I wanted. We should sleep in the bridge one last night before heading out to the cargo hold. But I was outvoted. I suppose getting rescue supplies is a better idea, but it will be hard to know what to bring if we don't know what we're walking into.I glance over at Evie. She rides atop the back of the alpha, Axyll, like some primitive warrior princess. I can't wrap my head around how quickly she has acclimated to the Celetans and their ways, how easily she navigates and has adjusted to the snow and cold weather.

Perhaps it has to do with the astrostingents Katie mentioned when we landed, the ones we're breathing now that we're outside of the filters of the ship. Maybe they help keep their host warm. Regardless of it, I eye Evie with a twist in my stomach. Is it envy? Is it anger? I'm not sure what this feeling is. Maybe it's disappointment she's accepted our fate so easily. The alpha called her his *mate*, and she does have a lovey-dovey glow about her. She's resigned to our desolate position and is ready to settle down on the planet. It seems too quick. I can't fathom it.*Maybe I can change her mind. When we get to the cargo hold, or find the fighter pod, we can scrap it for parts and figure out a way to send a message to the Miner's Association, or even the Intergalactical Alliance or a Terran Embassy...* The thought stops and I bite my bottom lip. I suppose it's not up to me to decide what is best for Evie, only for my crew. Only for those I'm responsible for. And me? I'm not staying here on this frozen wasteland—not if I can help it.

My gaze turns back to the enormous wolf pulling the sled. Juk. All of the Celetans are large, whether in their humanoid or wolf form, but Juk is easily distinguishable as the biggest. I only recognize the alpha because of Evie on his back, and there is one that is quite smaller than the others—a runt maybe?—but the other three all look the same to me. They're indistinguishable at this point, just large masses of muscle and white fur. With a third eye. I recognize Juk as the wolf I saw yesterday. He's the reason Evie was able to find us, and for that I am grateful. I only hope they'll be just as efficient at finding the cargo hold and the others. The fact that the cargo hold straddles enemy territory might be a problem, but I won't accept failure as an option. Enemy pack or not, I *will* find my missing four crew members.

There's the sound of a wolf howl in the distance, a small yip that means little to me. The sled stutters for a moment as Juk starts to slow. Suddenly, a blur of white launches out from the rock to our right. Katie lets out a scream, and my heart plummets as I watch a wolf tackle Evie off Axyll's back. He seems caught off guard, and before he can react, she's dragged away by the other wolf. Juk whimpers, and somehow, I know it's a question. One of the other indistinguishable wolves makes some sort of grunting sound, and Axyll responds with a sharp snap. Spittle flies from his mouth, and he races off after Evie and the attacking wolf. One of the other wolves from our group runs ahead of Juk, and the sled is pulled forward again as the giant beast pushes on.

"Wait! We need to go after them!" I shout. A knot forms in my stomach, and my pulse deafens my ears.

But my shouts are ignored, and we continue. Katie cries quietly into my shoulder, and I tighten my arm around her. Maybe the rival packs *will* be a problem.

After what feels like another two hours or so, we slow as we approach the bottom of a cliff. I spot movement above on a platform, and note the rungs dug into the ice along the cliff's face front. The wolves disappear around a bend, and Juk drops the pulley for the sled. He glances at me before disappearing with the others. Katie's cries have stopped, and I can feel Melanie shivering on the other side of her.

There is no sign of Axyll and Evie. My mind replays the other wolf ripping her off the alpha's back, and files it next to the sound of Chunhua's snapping neck, locking it away with the others that I've failed. The others who have died under my care. I'm not sure if Evie falls under my care, per se, but I feel like I have failed her. I was helpless and did not fight hard enough to go after her. I should have jumped out of the sled, but instead I stayed, frozen from shock.

The feeling eats away inside of me. But now that we've stopped, maybe it's not too late to do something about it. I ignore the faint snapping of bones sounding from around the corner and stand in the sled.

"Where are you going?" Katie asks. Melanie's teeth chatter next and she huddles closer into the furs.

"I'm going to get some answers," I say. "We need to go back for Evie."

I jump out of the sled and sink into the snow. It goes up to just past my knees, which does not surprise me. I may be the leader of my crew, but I am short. I won't let it stop me though.

As I begin to push my way through the snow towards the faint bone snapping, Juk comes around the corner. He's the tallest alien I have ever seen. There are a number of species who reside on Gragon 6, so I am used to seeing different beings frequently. There's a large community of Xlatians on Gragon 4, and Gragon 7 is mostly Trivsti communities. The Trivsti people are all over six feet, but Juk puts even them to shame.

His bright blue eyes find mine immediately and lock onto them. My heart flutters as he barrels towards me. He's nothing but rippling turquoise skin stretched across defined muscle. As he walks, he seamlessly swipes his light blonde hair up and ties it into a perfect bun at the top of his head. The gem in his forehead sparkles the closer he gets to me, and something about his look brings heat to my cheeks.

"Heyo!" calls a voice from up on the ridge. Both of us pause, our eye contact breaking as we look up. A blue figure waves down at us as another starts to descend the rungs towards the sled. The standing one shouts something down that I don't understand, and Juk responds in their native language.

"We need to go back and rescue Evie," I demand. Juk glances at me. Comparatively, he is a mountain and I am a tree. I barely come up to his pecs, which are bare and tantalizing. They shouldn't be, for I have no interest in getting cozy with the locals. I won't be catty and judge Evie about it like Melanie did, but I won't let anything distract me from saving the rest of my crew. Not even bright, teal pecs.

"The alpha commanded us to return to the den," Juk says to me in Terran English, dismissively. He takes an easy step around me and starts towards the sled.

I turn around, struggling. The snow is seeping through the black fabric of my mining suit, soaking my calves. I guess it's not waterproof. The other shifted men come out from their spot behind me. Two of them walk past, heading to the sled to help unpack, and one of them stops. He too, towers over me, but not at the same rate as Juk. His hair is cropped short all around, except for a long piece that flops into his light blue eyes.

"Do you need help through the snow?" he asks kindly as I sink in another foot while attempting to follow the others. His tails wag behind him and there is a smile plastered on his face.

I ignore him and call after Juk. "Your alpha doesn't command me. I'm in charge of these women and am responsible for them—we need to go back for Evie!"

Juk turns back around. He nods at the kind one beside me, who sighs and brushes past me to help Katie and Melanie out of the sled. The two of them are huddled together, the unfamiliar Celetans speaking at them in their language.

"In the star, Ee-vee said neither of you were in charge," Juk says. *Star? Is that what they think the ship is?* "And now you fall under the protection of the Snowscape Pack. Which means, *yes*, you take commands from the alpha. And when the alpha is not present? You take commands from me."

I blink, taken aback. Something thrums inside me, electrified by the command in his voice. The confidence and no-nonsense tone. I like it. In another life, we would get along great. But right now? He's standing in my way.

"The alpha will save her from Joval," Juk continues. He stands before me and starts to push the snow out with his legs. He's creating a path for me. I'm too annoyed to be thankful and I ignore the flutter in my chest.

"Who is Joval?" I ask as I follow him back to the sled. I see Katie tentatively stand in it and look over in my direction. She's too nervous without me there. I hate to admit it's much easier to walk through the snow with the makeshift path Juk is creating. I wonder if they have snowshoes here.

"He is the alpha's uncle."

"And he's dangerous?" I ask. Juk hesitates. We stop just before the sled. One of the Terran-speaking Celetans helps

Katie out of the sled, and the cheerful one with the short hair helps Melanie.

"No," he says at last. "But he has always been at odds with the alpha. Perhaps the arrival of his mate has caused those odds to turn into something darker."

Noted, I think as I turn and reach out to Katie. She rushes over to me, sticking to my side like glue. Melanie even shoots me an uneasy look from the other side of the sled. The cheerful Celetan is chatting her ear off, but it's clear to me she's not listening. Both women are looking to me for guidance. *I'm in charge of these women*, I repeat to myself. Melanie may be a pain in the ass, but she's under my care now. And it sounds like the dangers these Celetans harbour don't just come from outside of the pack—they come from the within too.

LISA

The Snowscape den is a giant cave. It sits on top of the plateau, carved into the mountain behind it at the top of the cliff. I keep my arm around Katie as we follow Juk and one of the others into the cave. Melanie stays close beside me. We pass a large circle of stones just outside the front of the cave, the outline of a large bonfire. There are drums set to one side next to three crude, carved stone stools.

I am surprised by the enormity of it as we are led inside. The tall rock walls carve upward towards a high ceiling. From far above there are scatters of light, cracks and crevices in the mountain above us. The smoke from a central fire trails up and out of sight, leaving the air crisp and clean inside. A few

Celetans wave at us from where they sit on the stone steps leading down to the fire pit.

While I expected a primitive cave, this is not what I pictured. As they call it a "den," I imagined everyone would be huddled together on the floor in a big pile. Maybe I pictured them living as wolves, preferring that form over their other. But instead, I find myself a bit impressed.

There is a blue hot spring glowing off to the left behind the fire. And all around, trailing down further into the cave, are smaller carved out living spaces. One does not picture individual homes when thinking of a wolf pack. There are no wolves on Gragon 6, but there are other animals that live in a similar hierarchy.

Three young toddling children go running to someone behind us. I glance over my shoulder and see one of our travel companions scoop up all three and swing them around in the air. Their shrieks and giggles echo through the cave. Despite how angry I want to be, despite how annoyed I am we need to wait another day to go rescue the others, the sight is heartwarming. It calms something in me, and a smile threatens to spread across my face.

A female Celetan follows the children. She smiles and nods her head at us but keeps a respectable distance as she catches up. The male—Amble, I think his name is? I remember it being something unusual—leans down and places a kiss on her cheek. He hands her one of the three children, and they begin talking in their language. They glance over to us and it's no mystery what they're talking about.

"Come, this way," Juk says. I take my eyes off the couple and glance over at him. His eyes find mine immediately, and there is a brief flash of light in the gem on his forehead. I want to blame it on a reflective light somewhere, but it's not the first time I've seen it happen. *Evie might be fine with settling down here, finding love in seven days, but I'm not. I won't.*

"Where are you taking us?" Katie whispers. Her voice cuts through my thoughts and startles me in its softness. Something in Juk's expression softens as he looks at her, at the fear and uncertainty in her eyes.

"To the healer. She will want to ensure you're unharmed," he explains.

I want to argue that we're fine. That we're not the ones who need the healer, but those in the cargo hold will. There was only one chair in there with a seatbelt. Gabby was strapped to it last I saw, and for all we know, she could be the only one alive. With her injured leg, I do not think she would last long. It's only by a miracle that the others would have survived with nothing to hold on to.

But then Katie nods her head and starts to move forward. And I remember she collapsed when she first tried to stand after the crash. She's been acting fine ever since, but maybe she's been hiding her pain, trying to stay strong so she can find her sister.

I nod and Juk leads us past a row of dwellings. There are even some on a second level, like an apartment building. Some have hides stretched across the entrances as makeshift doors, while others have the hides tied back with leather strips.

As we walk, a pack of wolf-life dogs come running up to us. They are much smaller than the Celetans in their wolf form, but larger than any canine I know of on Gragon 6. They're white, with only one tail and two eyes. One jumps up on Melanie and its long, purple tongue gives her a fierce lick.

"Yeck!" she squeals. Brex, the short-haired Celetan, laughs and calls the creature off her. He rubs its head, where I notice two spindly blue horns protruding out of its fur. Melanie glares at the thing. Brex doesn't notice. He continues to rub the creature's head between his hands in a very familiar owner-and-beloved-pet motion, and then he turns and flashes Melanie a smile.

"What are those?" Katie asks quietly. I know she's mentally adding the animal to the tally of creatures in her head.

"They are lupens," Brex says with a smile. The lupen barks in response. It sounds a bit like a honk, much different than the sounds the Celetans were making earlier in their wolf form. "This is Beska."

Beska barks again at her name. There are three others hanging around her, all a smaller size. Her pups or wards.

Juk leads on, and I squeeze past the horde of lupens. Katie continues to cling to my arms, but there is a spark of fascination in her eyes as she watches the group of animals run off.

"Does everyone have a lupen companion?" Katie asks.

Juk shakes his head. "No, not everyone."

We stop in front of one of the smaller cave dwellings. The leather flap is tied back, welcoming us inside. Before we even step a foot in, a woman pops her head out of the cave. She smiles brightly at us, the gem on her forehead shimmering. She is a foot shorter than Juk, and yet she still towers over me. If she is considered short among her people, I wonder how obscure our little group looks.

The woman turns and speaks to Juk in their native language. She looks a few years older than us, maybe late 20s by Terran terms. Her long, white hair is pulled back into various braids, and she wears a leather tunic over a set of leather leggings. Her light blue eyes sparkle with excitement as she turns to us and beckons us into her home.

"This is Nyfer," Juk explains as we enter the smaller cave.

There is a small, warm fire crackling to our left. Shelves are carved into the stone in a small alcove near the back, and there are four distinct beds made from piles of fur. Nyfer reaches out towards us, gesturing towards the bed closest to the fire.

"She would like to examine you," Juk explains.

Katie squeezes my arm tighter. Melanie makes no effort to move. I sigh and untangle myself from Katie's grasp as I move forward. Best to get this over with so we can move on with the preparations to rescue the others.

I sit down on the bed of furs. Nyfer kneels beside me.

"*Syht sy Leesa*," Juk says.

"*Lee-eesa*," Nyfer tries. I nod. It's good enough.

With gentle, blue hands, she reaches out to me. She rolls up one of my sleeves and places her hands on my arm. They are surprisingly warm, and instantly I feel comforted. It's the weirdest sensation. I can feel my heartbeat calm, and for a moment, the echoes of Chunhua and Delphine's death disappear from my mind. It is clear and free from the trauma.

The gem on her head sparkles. As I watch her close her eyes and the gem sparkle more, as I sneak a glance over to Juk, and think the Celetans have to be one of the most beautiful alien species I've encountered. Blue skin, white blonde hair, with high cheek bones, and mesmerizing blue eyes, the gems are the icing on top of the cake. Even their tails, which they keep in their human form, are a unique feature that is not unappealing.

Nyfer opens her eyes. She turns and speaks to Juk. His eyes stay on me, an intense stare I do not understand. My stomach flips over itself more than once, but I can't seem to break the eye contact either.

"She says you are uninjured, other than a little malnourished," he says at last. I stand as Nyfer gently pulls Melanie over next. "She says you should rest for a few days."

I scoff. "Not going to happen. We're leaving tomorrow to find the others."

The side of Juk's mouth twitches, as though he is amused. There is a chorus of loud shouts outside in the main cave suddenly, but it is unimportant.

"It will take a few days to gather rescue supplies," Juk says. "Tomorrow is too soon."

My hand curls into a fist. Apprehension swirls in my stomach, and the snap of Chunhua's neck echoes somewhere in my head. "A *few days* is too long. They've already gone six days without food or water."

"You do not know that for sure. Maybe they are resourceful," Juk says.

"They're injured!" I snap. "They had no safety precautions when their part of the ship ripped off!"

The room falls silent save for the fire crackling next to us. Nyfer's hands are on Melanie's arms, but her eyes move between me and Juk. My heart thumps in my chest, my desperation to get to the others bubbling too close to the surface.

I take a deep breath, willing the anger, the desperation to simmer down. My eyes close as I regain my composure, and when I open them, Juk's intense stare is still on me. His gem does that brief flash again, and somehow, I know only I can see it.

"Evie is right—there is no leader among all of us. But six of us were kidnapped together. Katie and I come from a group of women who work together, where *I* am their leader. I am responsible for them. I need to get to the other four lost out there. As soon as possible—please."

Juk towers over me as he takes a step forward. Nyfer closes her eyes again, her hands still on Melanie and her gem shines. Melanie faces the fire, her eyes lost in the flames as they glow on her pale cheeks. My heart pounds as I stare up, up, up at the tall Celetan, feeling like an ant among giants.

"I shall speak to the alpha and see what we can do," Juk says at last.

"The alpha? I thought he ran off to save Evie from that deranged wolf," Melanie mutters.

Juk glances at her before turning to me again. His hand next to his side twitches, and his tails swish ever so slightly. "It seems they have returned."

Melanie gets the same diagnosis as me: fine, albeit malnourished. She was taken by the Skulchers much earlier than I, so that does not surprise me. Katie is the same, but Nyfer mentions she is recovering from a head injury. A concussion, I assume.

"I don't remember hitting my head upon impact or anything," Katie says later. With tentative fingers, she reaches up and brushes her forehead, and then shrugs. "They seem like friendly people."

We've been shown to a cave—hollow, the Celetans call it—where the three of us will bunk together.

I nod, watching Katie carefully as though she may collapse again at any moment. I checked her for signs of a concussion when she first awoke, but there were none. *At least, I'm positive there weren't any. Are all my leadership skills suddenly slipping through my fingertips? Have I failed Katie too?*

"I'm very curious about the gems on their foreheads," Katie continues. "I didn't want to be rude and ask outright what they are."

"I'm sure you'll have lots of time to learn everything—not like we can leave this place," Melanie mutters as she rearranges a roll of furs given to her. Katie and I have placed our beds close together, but Melanie chooses another spot on the other side of the fire.

I want to retort to her pessimism, tell her that *no*, I am planning on getting off this planet. I don't know how, but this can't be the end for us here. But without a plan in place, there is no point in calling out Melanie's negative attitude.

Katie and Melanie fall asleep quickly that night. But for me, it is elusive.

My body is restless as I toss and turn, waking every moment that sleep is within my grasp. It makes no sense, as the stacked furs on the floor are the comfiest I've been since the Skulchers took us. I didn't think they would make that much of a difference, and thought I would miss the cold, hard floor of the spaceship. But my body is relaxed and cozy in these furs. If only my mind would relax as well.

With every close of my eyes, I hear the creak of the ship. I hear the screams of the women in the cargo hold echoing as we're ripped apart and as they plummet to the earth. I hear the snap of Chunhua's neck, and the blast into Delphine's back. I hear the whimpers and fear of the women who survive as we're led into the Skulchers' ship, the cry from Gabby as she falls and twists her leg, of Katie crying every night since we crashed landed here.

All because I couldn't protect them, I think. My leadership skills were too weak. Too slow. I couldn't save Chunhua and Delphine. I was too proud, too excited to be on the only all female-led crew in the Miner's Association to think about how that news would spread, and what targets that would put on our back. What was a great opportunity for us was a great opportunity for someone else—for different reasons.

And now we're here, I think as I stare up at the rocky ceiling. Katie sleeps soundly beside me, curled up in the furs.

Melanie lies nearby, her back to the fire. She's been oddly quiet since we got to the Snowscape den. It *is* a reprieve from her constant negative griping in the ship, but the sudden silence worries me. Apparently, I've taken her under my wing as well, without even meaning or knowing to. I will need to check in on her later.

The restlessness gets to be too much. I stand, careful not to disturb Katie next to me. She murmurs something in her sleep but does not stir. The fire next to us is safely banked, the flames low. I stare into the flames for a moment, debating if I should just stay here and sit awake. But my legs want to stretch. I want to move, to be active, to be doing *something* other than just waiting around.

I slip out behind the leather flap across the cave's entrance as quiet as possible. The main cave is quiet, but not silent. As I walk down the pathway towards the central fire, there are whispers and snores that come through the flaps of the other hollows. There is no one else out in the large cavern. The water from the hot spring reflects up onto the walls and ceiling, dancing from a self-illuminating source that I do not understand. It's beautiful and mesmerizing.

I'm tempted to strip and take a dip. The Celetans do not seem to have a problem with nudity. Earlier I spotted people coming and going into the pool unabashed. I'm not shy about my body, but it would be nice to take a dip in private, in the quiet reverie as I try to relax my addled mind and focus on what needs to be done.

I hover near the pool, debating, when something catches the corner of my eye. The flickering glow of flames, not from the central fire to the left of the hot spring, but coming from outside. I recall the circle of stones outside of the cave, and curiosity gets the better of me.

Something sharp and painful hits my gut as I approach the entrance. The feeling comes from within me, a bitter mix of betrayal, hurt, and—dare I admit—jealousy. My shoulders tense as I lean against the cave's entrance and watch the scene before me.

The two moons are bright and glorious. The larger one—Vekao, I think—dwarfs the smaller one. Vekao is just past being full. Its bright light shines over everything in front of me, and the bright white of its light reminds me so much of Gravion it hurts. I will never see that star again, will never see any of the eight Gragon colonies that circle around it.

Don't think like that, I spit internally at myself. *We'll get off this planet. We'll get back to Gragon 6...*

But is it even safe there? Look at what happened, a wiser, quiet piece of me whispers. I ignore it.

My jaw hardens as I look past the dancing flames of the outdoor bonfire. I know from its size it's not nearly as big as it could be. Not as big as it would be if this display were on show for everyone in the pack. This scene I've stumbled upon is private. Not necessarily a secret, but something quiet just for the two of them. And it makes me angry.

Axyll and Evie stand before the fire, their hands clasped together. I don't need to understand Nyfer's words to know what's going on. This is a bonding ceremony. A marriage, a uniting, whatever it may be called in this culture. Evie has given up. It's no longer about survival for her. After we find the others, she intends to *stay* here.

Not like we can leave the planet, Melanie's sneering words echo in my head. My heart beats rapidly at the thought. The hairs on the back of my neck stand on end, and something starts to eat me from the inside. *Failure. You couldn't keep them safe. Any of them. Two are dead, and now the rest of you will rot away on this uncharted planet, in nothing but ice and cold.*

"I guess we won't all be cold and lonely," I mutter aloud, barely a whisper. Evie laughs at something the alpha says, and my blood starts to boil. I defended her actions to Melanie, that coupling with this guy was a means of survival. But it's clear I'm wrong. It's developed into something more. Something *permanent* in Evie's eyes.

Next to Nyfer is a woman's name who I don't remember. One of the elders, I think. She smiles happily at Axyll and Evie. And next to her is Juk.

His bright blue eyes find me the minute I lean against the entrance. And they stay on me as my shoulders tense and my teeth grind watching the ritual. I know I don't have any say in what Evie chooses for her future. I wish I knew why it bothered me so much. Maybe it's because I'm hellbent on finding a way off this planet. There must be something we can do to get the ship operational again. This can't be our end destination.

Or maybe it's because, deep down, I know she and Melanie are right. We're stuck here. Even if we returned to Gragon 6, how long would it be before another crew of Skulchers scooped us up? We aren't safe there.

A shiver runs down my spine as Juk's gaze on me is unwavering. The moonlight catches his blonde hair, a darker shade than everyone else's white-blond, but still a bright gold colour. A strand has escaped the usual bun he has swept up on the top of his head, and tickles his cheek.

The woman starts to chant and sing something in time with Nyfer. Juk keeps his eyes locked on mine, and another shiver runs through me. And I know it's not from the cold.

I push away from the entrance, my eyes on him, just as unwavering. Daring him to break the contact first. My heart pounds and my hands curl into fists at my side. My nails dig into my palm as I force myself to focus on the feeling there, on the scrape as they rip into my skin. Because I refuse to feel the heat that is starting to pool in my core. The flutter of my heart at the intensity in his eyes.

Finally, Juk looks away as Nyfer grabs his attention back to the ceremony. His voice joins the chants, and the low rumble of it follows me in back through the entrance into the den.

I let my shoulders relax as I make my way back to the hollow. Let Evie become united with Axyll. Let her stay on the planet. Let her give up.

It's the last thing on my mind.

LISA

DAY 8

"I'm not going."

Melanie's words do not surprise me. She crosses her arms and refuses to make eye contact with anyone in the hollow.

We are crammed inside Axyll—and Evie's—hollow. As alpha, he likely has one of the bigger living spaces, but with three Celetans and four humans inside, space is limited around the fire.

Katie stands next to me, her shoulder brushing against mine. Melanie stands on the other side of her, keeping a personal bubble around her between Katie on her one side and Brex on her other. Juk stands next to Axyll and Evie across the flames.

Evie nods her head at Melanie's words. She glances uncertainly at me, and I shrug. Melanie is not part of my crew. If she wants to stay behind, she can. I think Katie should stay behind too, but don't mention it as I know she won't agree. She wants to come to find her sister.

"That's fine, you can stay here with the pack," Axyll says firmly.

"I shall stay too, if you agree Alpha," Brex says a little too eagerly. His tails swish back and forth. Melanie shoots daggers at him as one of them brushes up against her leg, and she shuffles closer to Katie.

Axyll raises his eyebrow at Brex but only for a moment. He nods in agreement. "Yes. One beta should stay behind. Brex, you can stay behind unless Juk would prefer—"

"I do not," Juk interrupts. His eyes flicker over to me, so quickly I'm certain I imagined it. Brex tries to hide a smile, his tails wagging harder. I hope Melanie can handle herself while we're gone.

"Good," Axyll continues. "Brex can stay behind with the females—"

"The rest of us are coming," I say. "I thought that was clear."

Axyll looks up at me, annoyance written on his features from being interrupted again. The pack hierarchy must be pretty totalitarian, for it's clear this guy is used to being in charge. Things are about to change if he thinks he's bringing a bunch of humans into the pack.

"Or, I should say, Katie and I are going for sure," I continue. Best not to piss off the alpha of the pack trying to save us. To keep us safe, housed, and fed. "I won't speak for Evie."

"Jade is out there," she says with a sigh. "I want to make sure she's OK. She became pretty attached to me once the Skulchers brought her into the cell. I want to make sure the others are OK too."

There's something about the way she says it that feels like a dig to me. Like because I have my crew as number one priority it means I wouldn't help the others. Maybe she's right. Or maybe I'm reading into it too much. The knot of failure in my gut twists and turns, and I feel like nothing makes sense anymore.

"If you are sure," Axyll says softly as he turns to look at Evie. He strokes her cheek with one of his blue fingers, and her brown eyes soften. They glow with an adoration that makes my back tense again. *Let her have her happy ending. They're helping us find the others. It'll be OK.* Something makes me glance over at Juk, who is looking at me again. I turn away.

"I'm sure," Evie says.

"OK. Brex will stay here with the pack, and *Meelany*," Axyll says. Melanie's name is lost on them. "The rest of the *Teerans* will come with us to rescue the others—"

"Humans. Not all of us are Terrans," I interject.

Axyll tilts his head curiously and exchanges a look with Juk. He then turns to Evie.

"Oh, sorry, I guess that was me," she says. She scratches the back of her neck and gestures with her other hand to us across the fire. "*Terran* is the term mostly used by those of us from Terra. Some other species use it interchangeably, but it's not wrong. We're all *humans*, but we come from different planets."

"Like different packs?" Brex asks.

"Sort of, I guess," Evie shrugs.

I sigh, regretting I mentioned it as now we're off topic. There's no point in explaining that Katie and I are Gragians, and Melanie is a Lagustan. "Let's get back on track. Evie, Katie, and I are coming along for the rescue."

Axyll nods, though there is still a quizzical look on his face. "We will take Hazen, Baz, Tabros, and Kalpa with us."

"That's it?" I ask. "There are seven women in that cargo hold."

"Juk will pull our largest sled with supplies for everyone. Kalpa can pull the other already assembled. We are taking two deltas with us, and one of our best hunters. This leaves only one beta, one delta, and three hunters to protect the rest of the pack. There are elders, females, and children here that need to be protected," Axyll explains. "If the *hoo-mans* are on the Snowscape side of the territory, then there will be no cause for trouble."

"And if they're on the other side?" Katie asks.

Axyll turns to her, his blue eyes suddenly dark. "Then we will need to reassess and prepare for a fight."

JUK

The wind is brisk, but the sun is high as I piece together the largest of our sleds. The various pieces have been brought down from the den, always a tedious task, and now my mind wanders as my hands assemble it together.

There is much to prepare for. Many unknown things and circumstances that we could be walking into. Food, furs, clothing, blankets, weapons, strips of leather for wounds... the list seems endless.

Kalpa mutters something angrily to himself a few metres away from me, and drops the stack of furs he carries to the smaller sled. He scoops them up, dusting the snow off them, before packing them carefully into the small sled.

I hide my grin as he glances over at me and continue about my work quietly. Kalpa is the youngest Celetan of rank, though Brex beats him only by one full rotation of seasons. A capable delta by any standard, he shares his sister's quick temper.

"It will be interesting to see the other females," he muses aloud as he reassesses his packing job, and adjusts the bundle of furs.

My hands move swiftly, piecing together the large bone frame. The bones are from a strostk, a large woolly beast that roams the eastern plains in our territory. They are peaceful creatures, traveling in small herds that flatten the land wherever they go. It is not often we hunt them, for their meat is thick and unsavoury, but every once in a while we bring one down when needed.

The bones and thick hide are used for sleds, while the meat is dried and stored for emergency rations. I have only been on one strostk hunt, but as I begin to tie the leather sides of the sled into place, I wonder if another one is due. With so many new females coming into our pack, into our care, there will be more mouths to feed. More clothes to make, more furs needed for beds, more bone cups and bowls, more fires to tend and stock...

"It will be a lot of work," I say at last, for I know Kalpa waits for an answer. He is quick to temper, but he is also a talker. Unlike his sister, Jenneka. That is where they differ.

Kalpa scoffs. "You are not curious about them? About the idea of a mate, of more litters born to the Snowscapes? Our pack growing?"

I think of Axyll and Ee-vee the night before. Their uniting ceremony was beautiful, I do admit, but I am still in shock.

That my alpha would find a mate so quickly, and with someone so different. That his Seeker would call out to her upon their first meeting... and that mine would do the same.

My eyes glance up towards the ridge. From this angle, I cannot see the entrance to the den. I cannot see the circle of stone that banks the bonfire. I can only see the rungs leading up to our home carefully hidden in the icy rock of the cliff. But I can picture her. Dark hair, fierce eyes, and pursed lips as she watched from the entrance last night. My hearts pulsed, my Seeker shone, and if Nyfer had not interrupted me, I would have never looked away.

I am a hypocrite to question my alpha's new choice of mate, when my Seeker, too, has chosen one of new *Teerans*. A gift from Vekao indeed, the first sight of her on top of the fallen star, throwing balls of snow down at me...

No, that is not right, I remind myself. *They are hoo-mans. Only Evie comes from the Teeran Pack.*

"I do not like the idea of being so close to Stygian territory," I say at last. There is no need for me to be curious about the other females—my fated one is already here.

Kalpa cocks his head thoughtfully. A strand of his white hair blows into his face, but he makes no move to brush it aside. My fingers itch at the thought of my hair in my face, getting in the way. More than once I have thought of shearing it short like Brex wears his, but I cannot bring myself to do it.

"What if Vekao brought the females to the territories as a sign of change? It is no secret the packs are suffering, are becoming smaller. Fewer litters being born with females... what if Vekao delivered the females on the Stygian border as a gift for both packs?" Kalpa muses. "Perhaps it is a chance for both packs to thrive and grow anew."

My fur bristles at the idea of Leesa mating with a Stygian. My hearts beat wildly at the thought, the drumming of it in my ears drowning out all other sound. I glance up again at the plateau, my Seeker shining mildly knowing she is up there somewhere. *No. She is mine. She is meant for me.*

"Then what of the Ashen Pack?" I ask, only to amuse myself with his fantasies.

Kalpa snorts. "The Ashen Pack are unnatural. They can fall apart while the true packs survive."

"You should keep your delusions to yourself," I say. "Vekao would never send a gift to the Stygians."

"Then why did the females arrive in stars?" Kalpa counters. His curious mind is trying my patience this day.

"To warn them that their time is ending," I say confidently. "And to strengthen the Snowscape Pack. The females will be on our side of the territory line, of that I am sure."

As Kalpa shrugs and continues packing supplies into the smaller sled, I turn back to my sled assembly.

At the very least, my female is. And that is all that matters.

LISA

There is a lot to prepare for. I will give the Celetans credit for wanting to be prepared for all scenarios. I want to complain about it taking too long; I want to demand that we leave today, that there is little time that can be spared, that we must get to the others *now*. But I cannot. The Celetans work tirelessly to get everything ready.

Everyone pitches in. And I mean *everybody*. The elders rip long strips out of leather for bandages, and the young children help roll them up. The healer and her daughter prepare various salves and elixirs, packaging them in skin pouches and carved bone jars. Two other women pack dried meat into hide bags, stuffing them as full as possible. The hunters then go out to catch fresh kills to replenish the caches that we are emptying for our journey.

Katie and I are outfitted in new gear. Katie more so than myself. Evie's blue coveralls provide little warmth, and her original miner's outfit was destroyed when Evie was attacked. Now, Katie wears a pair of leather leggings, and a tunic with long sleeves. We both have new boots lined and trimmed with fur, but I still don my miner's suit. The material is thin but weather resistant, and will keep me warm enough. I refuse to let it go, likening the action as to giving up. Katie had no choice given her suit was wrecked, but I will not assimilate into the pack. We are getting off this planet.

We help out everywhere we can. We take rolled up furs from the storage hollow and pass them down to Juk and Kalpa who are packing the sleds. We help melt snow over the fire and fill the leather pouches they use as canteens with water for the first day of the journey. We pack extras for those in the cargo hold.

I try to think of who I know is resourceful in the group there. I know my four are. Allison is fierce. I know she will be eager to find us, to find Katie. But she won't leave the others behind to do it. She'll want them to stick together, and with Gabby's busted leg, they're likely staying put. They should each still have their issued flints and can start a fire. If not, I'm sure that the fighter—Raegan—is resourceful. Anyone who has been a captive of the Skulchers and stuck on their planet *has* to be a survivor. Maybe one day I'll learn her story.

Beyond that, I don't know much about the other two women there. We were only with them for three days before our escape and crash onto the planet. Jade was very timid, I remember that. She stuck to Evie like glue, which is why the alpha's new mate wants to come with us to find everyone else. And I don't remember anything about the last woman.

It's a long day. Even as the sun starts to set, and the bright glow of the giant moon takes over the sky, everyone is still working. It's a quieter hush now, with the children put to sleep. Katie, Evie, and I sit close to the large central fire, sifting through a small pile of clothing that the female Celetans have given to us for those in the cargo hold.

"I think these will fit Jade," Evie says as she holds up a pair of leggings. They're a pair donated by the healer's daughter, who is about the same height as me. Jade is short too, I remember that.

Evie folds up the leggings and puts them on top of a smaller tunic she's picked out for the timid human. She then reaches for a pair of boots, shakes her head and puts them back into the pile. Nobody will get a perfect fit of anything until they can be brought back here and tailored. It's another nail in the coffin that this is where we're trapped, possibly for the end of our days, that I try to ignore. I don't appreciate my mind pointing these things out to me, when I'm so clearly determined to get off the planet.

We have an outfit for Allison already picked out, easy as she's the same size as Katie, and another for Chelsea. Katie and I work on finding something that will fit Gabby's curves, while Evie finishes Jade's pile and moves onto Raegan or Navi.

Melanie sits off to the side, not helping. She hasn't done much of anything today except either stay in our hollow or follow us around like a shadow, her only other movement the incessant twisting of the delicate silver chain around her neck. The motion is familiar to me, as she did the same thing the entire time we were in the bridge. I want to slap her hands away and tell her there are more important things than her stupid necklace, but I can recognize a nervous habit. Chunhua used to do something similar, and the reminder makes my heart squeeze.

Katie stifles a yawn as she holds up a pair of leggings. They are a bit short for Gabby, I think, but they'll fit her curves. I reach out and take them from her, folding them neatly. We can wrap the exposed part of her legs with bits of fur and tuck it into her boots.

"You should get some rest," I say as Katie stretches her arms over her head, another yawn escaping. "It's going to be a long day tomorrow."

"We should all get some sleep," Evie says as she finishes her clothing bundles. She stacks the piles all together and stands. "I'll bring these to Axyll. I think he's doing a final check over the sleds, and then I'm going to bed. I'll see you in the morning."

As Evie walks towards the den's entrance, Brex comes striding in. He spots us over by the fire, two large rabbit-looking creatures strung over his shoulders. Tails waggling like a happy dog, he waves over at us—at Melanie specifically—as he comes over.

Melanie shifts uncomfortably, her lips in a thin line. She pulls the pale beige sweater she refuses to give up tighter around her.

"Are you sure you're going to be here OK by yourself?" Katie whispers as Brex makes his way over. The guy is clearly enamoured. I glance from him to Melanie, and need to suppress a groan. What is with all the human women falling for these guys? First Evie, and now Melanie? Maybe she actually *is* uncomfortable, but even with the glow of the fire trying to hide it, I can spot the blush colouring her cheeks.

"I don't have much of a choice, do I?" she snaps back quietly.

"You could come with us," I point out.

Melanie stands as Brex sits down. He's on the other side of the fire, giving us space. Manners aren't completely lost on these people, I'll give them that. The two dead critters land with a thud on the floor, and he brings out a bone knife to start slicing them up.

"I'm not going out there again," Melanie says. We stand with her and start to head back to our hollow. My limbs suddenly feel tired, the day's working catching up with me. But the rest of me feels wired. I'm ready to go and find my missing people. To find the rest of my crew and make sure they're OK—to be the leader I am supposed to be.

"You're just going to end up back here anyway," Melanie continues, the spite and sadness thick in her voice. "If you survive. No point in going out if this is the end game."

I open my mouth to argue, but Katie shoots me a look. It's one I'm familiar with, one she used often when the three of us were in the bridge. *We all process things differently*, I can hear Katie's soft voice say. *Some better than others. We're all stranded here, in a situation that is not ideal. Once the dust settles, I'm sure Melanie will become more pleasant.*

Somehow, I doubt it.

JUK

DAY 9

The next day, I am the first to rise in the pack. I slip out of my shared hollow, Brex still snoring loudly next to me and exit into the main cavern. The beta B was up late the night before, skinning the meat of his fresh kills to replenish the stores.

My skin ripples with anticipation. I stoke the central fire, waking the flames hiding low within the wooden fuel, bringing it back to life before I make my way outside. I can hear my alpha and his mate quietly mating in their cave as I near the entrance. One last moment of privacy before we are together for six days to travel to the territory's border.

Vekao greets me as I emerge from the den's entrance. She is luminous in the sky, which is painted with purples, greens, and the soft glow of yellow as the sun begs to break on the horizon. The stars still litter the sky, not yet drowned out by the sun's light, and the wind is still on this day. I see no clouds on the horizon, and yet my Seeker twitches in my mind.

I do not know what bothers it as I climb down the cliff's face to the base at the bottom. Amble sleeps down here in his celestial form, guarding the assembled and packed sleds. At the sound of my descent, his looks up lazily, Seeker gazing at me, before lowering his head again.

"I wish to have a quick run to stretch my legs before the others awake," I say quietly, knowing he can hear my words. The delta snuffs in response, his eyes still closed. His Seeker still gapes at me through a half-lid, guarding the sleds and our den.

As I shift quickly, bones snapping in and out of place, something small twists inside me. My intuition is warning me of something, but my Seeker cannot yet place what it is. Something about the upcoming trip, something not favourable.

Once shifted, I shake out my fur and stretch my front legs. I ensure that my scrap of leather is tied securely to my back leg. It is a treasured piece that I must have on me, always.

Then, I bound forward into the snow. I race past Amble, who does not bother to lift his head as I run by. My paws pound against the snow, large, but silent. The feeling reverberates through my body as I run at full speed, no destination planned. I merely mean to stretch my muscles, burn off my nervous energy, and clear my mind.

Kalpa's words from the day before ring through my mind. Thoughts of change and of our pack moving forward. Female Celetans are rare. They have always been rare, for as long as our ancestors can remember, going as far back to when Vekao gifted us our celestial forms. Some generations fared better than others, having what would be considered a plentiful bounty of females to bring forth the next line of litters.

But ours was one of the lower rated ones. And the sickness that swept through the territories did not help. Our previous alpha and his mate were lost, as were most of our parents' generation. They were lost either from the sickness, from the unspeakable cold that swept through, or from scraps with the other packs as resources and food grew sparse. The sickness started within the Ashen Pack and spread to the Stygians and Snowscapes.

Most of my generation was spared. The elders before us fought tirelessly to keep us from fever. Some were lost, such as Hant's littermates. And the five elders we have now are all that remain from the generation before us. *Four—four elders*, I remind myself. Joval has been exiled for his brash attack on the alpha's mate. I have never understood his hatred towards Axyll, a hatred started when the alpha was a young cub.

I push thoughts of Joval from my mind as the sun-kissed mountain air hits my face. Given how few females there are of my generation, two of whom have already born at least one litter each, perhaps Kalpa's thoughts are true. Maybe these strange, short, tailless females are meant to strengthen our pack. While there are still more unmated males than there are new *hoo-man* females, it does bring up our numbers. Brings up our chances to have more cubs, to continue the survival of the Snowscape Pack. Our alpha has already taken one as a mate, and though it is much, much too early to think on whether they can even *have* a litter of cubs, it is something. It is a possibility.

But more than half of these new females may reside in the Stygians' territory. The *Stygians*. My paws dig into the snow as I come to a halt. Overlooking the snow-covered valley, the endless peaks of mountains, some littered in the greens and blues of the trees, my hearts pound in my broad rib cage. Those dark-coated, amber Seeker, star-worshipping *heathens*... To think that Vekao would gift them the same as us, that she would gift them *more* than us... it is unfathomable. It is outrageous.

What have they done to deserve such a gift? Living underneath the mountains, roaming at night, worshipping the stars instead of Vekao's magnificent light—or even small Jaci's in comparison... There is nothing they deserve but a swift death. They are fierce, which is an admirable quality I suppose, but they are monsters. Vicious and unfeeling, our natural enemies since the beginning of time. There is no reason for Vekao to favour them, to gift them *more* females than the Snowscapes. One already lies in their mountains. But the others, the seven we set out today to rescue, they are meant for us. Not them.

An updraft from the cliff below me ruffles my fur, and snowflakes skitter into my nose. It is cold and abrupt, snapping me from my muddled thoughts. I give my head a shake and a sharp exhale to clear my mind once more.

It is not up to me to decide what is fair or not in the eyes of Vekao. She favours at her whim, and her plan is absolute. It is not for me to know her plan, only to follow the course she lays before me. If she has plans to aid the Stygians—for whatever pervert reason—then there is nothing to be done. And there are no signs showing favour towards the Ashen Pack.

I recognize the path laid before me, or so I think. My trek back to the den, back to where the others are rising with the sun, getting another quick meal in before it is time to depart, is slower. My mind is cleared now, the thoughts and unsettling questions thrown out as I focus on what I do know. What I have not yet accepted that Vekao has gifted me.

Leesa. The thought of her sends the breath out of me. I think of her slight frame, her dark eyes and hair, and of her determination to get back to her people. She is a leader, Leesa. The *hoo-mans* say they have no alpha among them, that they make their decisions together, but I am not so sure. Leesa has the spirit of a leader. She argues back against the alpha, she directs the two other new females who came to our den. She is demanding and fierce, and my hearts soar at the thought of her.

But she is not happy here. I do not need to ask her to know it. It is plain on her features, on the disdain written across her face when Axyll and Ee-vee were united under the moon. It fractures something inside me, ever so slightly. To know that Vekao has given me a mate, one that blinds my Seeker each time with her flawless presence, only for her to be unhappy here... how can one mate with someone like that?

Perhaps it is for the best. The idea of a mate has always been an anxious one for me. My duty as a beta is to protect my alpha at all costs. I see the conflict sometimes that Amble faces with his delta duties, and his urge to protect his family. I have been alone most of my life, and I have dedicated my life to protecting the pack. To suddenly have someone in my life who might distract my focus, to have to choose between protecting my alpha and protecting her... the thought is terrifying.

It is best if I do not have to choose at all. I will help Leesa find her people, and from there, I imagine they will return to the stars. My hearts will break when she leaves, when the glimmer of a family and cubs fades back into nothing but an unattainable dream. But it will be for the better. Ee-vee may have chosen to join our pack, but I will not force Leesa to do it. I do not even think she realizes that we are meant to be, that we are fated to be with one another... and I will not enlighten her of it.

LISA

"We will head to your *sheep* to give Tabros and Hazen the language beam," Axyll explains.

The plan has been explained again and again, with little alteration from the alpha. It makes sense for the two newcomers to get the language dump for when we find the other women. If we get separated or they're spread across a distance, then they can communicate if we get split up. It's a good plan, except for the part I don't like: spending the night at the ship.

I think it's a waste of time. Not the language part, necessarily, but spending another night there. It takes half a day's run for the Celetans in their wolf form to get to the ship. The language transfer takes only a few moments, with little recovery time. I don't like the idea of wasting daylight hours, but the alpha will not budge on this no matter how many times I argue against him.

So, I stay quiet as he confirms the plan again as we stand at the bottom of the ledge that houses their den. Katie nods her head next to me. She's bundled from head to toe in furs, nestled next to me in the big sled.

Evie stands next to the alpha, her hand clasped in his. Her eyes flicker to me, waiting to see if I'll argue against him, but I stay tight-lipped and keep my mouth shut. There's a flash of relief across her face, and I fight to keep the annoyance off mine. I don't understand how the urgency doesn't eat her alive like it does me. *Was she this laid-back when she was out looking for help? Did we become a second priority the moment she met Axyll?*

Something moves in the corner of my eye, and my heartbeat quickens. A large, white furred wolf approaches our large sled. His blue eyes lock with mine, the third one unblinking as it fixates on me.

Juk.

Those eyes see through me, stripping me down to my soul in a way that I cannot explain. They're the same eyes that watch me when he's human, when I involuntarily search for his towering form among the other Celetans. Even in wolf form, they cause goosebumps to appear on my arms, and heat to stir in my loins.

Not going to happen.

Whatever this feeling is, it disappears the moment I force myself to look away.

"I'll ride on Axyll's back to the ship," Evie says as she steps toward the sled. "Once we start the longer treks tomorrow, I'll ride in the sled with you two."

Katie nudges my side under the blankets when I don't answer her. "Sounds good," she responds on behalf of both of us.

Evie moves off to check the smaller sled, whose wolf is at the ready, pulley in his mouth. The wind carries the sound of Axyll's bones snapping from around the corner, and I flinch. I roll my shoulders and adjust the blankets to cover the reaction to the sound, a flash of Chunhua coming before my eyes. But when I blink again, I notice that Juk's eyes have narrowed on me as though my adjustment didn't fool him.

I look away again as the giant wolf turns, and picks up the pulley of our large sled. The alpha comes around the corner, his two main eyes looking over the group while the third eye locks on Evie. She climbs onto his back, warrior-princess style again.

The ride over to the ship goes smoothly. The faint sun shines down on us, illuminating the glittering snow. Katie is quiet beside me. I can see her glancing at me now and then. I keep my eyes trained forward, trying to organize my thoughts. They're a jumbled mess of urgency to reach the rest of my crew; of an odd, unsettling jealousy towards Evie that I don't understand; and the always present guilt over Chunhua and Delphine's deaths.

By the time we reach the ship, the sun is just over the peak of midday. The pack pulls up to the backside of the ship, leaving the sleds at a distance from the blue shield that acts as the door. Evie slides down from Axyll's back, and murmurs something as she pats his head. I wonder if the gesture is demeaning to him in some way, as it's like he's her pet. I can't help but glance over to Juk as the thought crosses my mind. He drops the sled's pulley in front of him, and wanders over around to the other side of the ship, away from us.

Is his fur soft? Is it wiry and coarse? Would he mind if I patted his head or scratched him behind the ears? *Would you even be able to reach his head?* I wonder, thinking of how towering he is and how short I am. *Would our height difference bother him?*

Katie's shifting body next to mine breaks me from the intrusive thoughts. Intrusive because I don't want to be thinking about them. I defended Evie and her actions, yes, but now every time I notice how enamoured she is, how settled she seems to be with the pack, I shudder. My stomach flips with protest, as settling down with these aliens is not the priority there. Falling for them is not an option, not so quickly, not when the other women are waiting for us. And yet, as Katie stands to climb down from the sled, and Juk comes back around the corner, back in human form with his hair swept back up and completely naked, I can't help but look over at him. And my heart squeezes.

"Guess their clothes don't shift with them, eh?" Katie whispers. Her cheeks are turning bright red as another of the Celetans, Hazen, comes around from the other end of the ship, also naked. They move over to the smaller sled where they promptly pull out folded pairs of leather pants, and slip into them before turning towards us.

"Guess not," I say. As Katie starts to climb out, I quickly grab her hand before the Celetans get to us. "We should sweep the ship one last time," I whisper quickly, "take a final look to see if there is any equipment we can bring that might be useful to send a signal. The cargo hold might have something else compatible."

Katie frowns. "I suppose we can look, but you know we've tried everything so far. Lisa, I know you don't want to give up, that you want to send a message to Gragon 6, but the Skulchers' tech is all junk. And I'm doubtful the cargo hold will have anything useful, and after its fall..."

"I know, I know," I hiss back quickly. Juk and Hazen speak to each other quietly nearby, still heading over. Axyll has gone around the corner to shift, as has another wolf, but the last one stays in wolf form. "But if we can find the escape pod, I think we can get a message to Gragon 6. I think we—"

I stop as Juk stands before us. Even standing tall in the sled, already a foot off the ground, he is still taller than me. He offers me his hand to help me climb down, but I don't take it. I push past Katie, and jump out of the sled, landing next to him. My feet sink deep into the snow. White powder clings around my calves as the snow comes up to my knees, and Juk gives me a puzzled look. Maybe I should have taken his offer of help, but it's too late now. The entrance to the ship is close by, and I stubbornly push through the high snow as Katie takes the offered hand instead.

As I reach the doorway and start to brush the snow off my legs, Juk comes rushing over. His large hand comes down onto my shoulder for a moment, stopping me from crossing over the threshold.

"Wait. Let me ensure the star remains undisturbed," he says. There's a shining in his eyes I don't understand but makes my stomach flip as he cautiously steps through the blue barrier and into the ship. A moment later he returns with a nod of his head. "It is safe to enter."

"Of course it is," I say as I push past him into the ship. The smell from the overflowing latrine has festered and oozes through the solid wall to my left. It's a stark reminder of the days spent living here, waiting to see if help would arrive. It feels like a lifetime ago, when it was only *two days ago.* Maybe it isn't Evie's fault she's moved on and content with her new situation. Maybe there is something about survival situations that make moving forward essential.

The bridge is undisturbed from how we left it. Signs of our living here are littered on the ground. A battered blanket we didn't bother to bring because it's falling apart, scraps of metal that were otherwise useless at the time but could maybe prove useful once we get to the cargo hold. I'll sift through it again later.

The windshield is nearly completely covered in snow. A meek light blinks on the console, warning us that the ship's power is low.

"I'll start to get the language transfer up and running," Katie says as she enters the bridge.

"I'll need to go clear the solar panel again," I say as I point towards the indicator. "The power is low."

"Looks like the charge isn't holding as well as it was," Katie says as she sits down at the console. "I'll see if I can fix that once it's up and running. I think the alpha would like to have the rest of the pack eventually get the language as well."

Not you too, Katie... thinking long term. I keep my thoughts and frown to myself. Instead, I nod and head back out into the snow. I catch the tail-end sound of bones snapping, and flinch. My eyes close, and I take a deep breath to steady the sudden quickening of my heart, and to push the mental image of Chunhua away. *Will it always haunt me?*

"Are you alright, Leesay?"

Axyll stands in front of me, Evie at his side. She gives me a worried look, and there is an odd shine coming off the gem in the alpha's forehead.

I nod. "Yes, I'm fine. I need to get on the roof to clear the solar panel. The ship is low on power, and we'll need it to charge a bit before we can do the language transfer for Hazen and...?"

"Tabros," Axyll reminds me.

"Tabros," I repeat.

"Let me help you," Evie says. I shrug in agreement. It's not a two-person job, but if it'll help her feel useful, I won't stand in her way.

"Is it safe?" Axyll asks, eyeing the roof of the ship warily.

"Leesa has been up there before—it is where we first met," Juk's deep voice states. Axyll moves to the side, and I see him there, leaning against the side of the ship. His teal skin is bright and stark against the white backdrop of the endless snow. His eyes, as always, seem to be on me. His gem shines brighter than Axyll's, but maybe it's just the angle of the sun.

"It's safe enough," I answer, tearing my gaze away from him and back to the alpha.

Axyll slowly nods his head. He then turns to Juk. "I will go hunt with Baz, then. We will have a fresh meal tonight, and smoke the rest for our travels. You stay here with Hazen and Tabros, and help the females with the ceiling spear. Hazen,

Tabros, go find branches for a fire while the females fix the ceiling spear."

"Yes, Alpha," Juk says without skipping a beat. His eyes stay on me.

I move past the alpha and Evie, not needing to see them tongue each other goodbye. The one Celetan still in wolf form stretches his legs, and nods his enormous head at his alpha, as though he can understand him. I guess the language recognition stays the same when in wolf form.

As Axyll moves away from the ship to shift back, I start to brush snow off the metal rungs on the side of the hull. Some are crunched in from when the ship scraped into the side of the mountain. A few are ripped right off. I briefly think of the mechanic woman, Meg, who climbed outside of the ship to fix the shield. She saved all of us who were inside the bridge from flying out to our deaths or suffocating from the lack of oxygen. I can't imagine being on the outside of the ship when Evie was flying wildly through the thick clouds, narrowly skimming against the snowy mountains.

The climb up to the roof is tricky, but I've done it a few times now. The bottom few rungs are the ones that are either warped or missing, and I need to go up on my tiptoes to reach the first one that is usable. The other option is to make a pile of snow to step onto the first rung, and reach better from there.

As I stretch my arms up to gage the distance between me and the first rung, a pair of large, strong hands land on my hips.

Before I can even react, I'm hoisted up into the air like I weigh little more than a pillow.

"What the—"

I look over my shoulder and down into Juk's neutral face. My heart beats rapidly in my chest, and for a moment I'm dazed. I can feel the warmth from his palms even through the fabric of my miner's suit. The gem in his forehead shines when I look at it. It's a pale colour against the vibrant teal of his skin.

I jerk myself up the rest of the way, tearing my gaze away from Juk. The snow is nearly up to my knees as I carefully trudge through it to the buried solar panels. From the corner of my eye, I see Juk lift Evie up the rungs as well. Out of my other corner, I see two massive white wolves take off at a jarring speed into the endless white snow.

"How are you doing?" Evie asks as she comes to my side. I know she's not talking about clearing off the panel, which is a one-person job.

I can't help the wave of annoyance that comes at her question. The twinge of jealousy I can't understand and refuse to analyze. The feel of Juk's hands still warm on my hips.

"The sooner we find the others, the better," I say as neutrally as possible. "Then we can figure out the next steps from there."

"I suspect Brex will be working on arrangements for the others, assigning hollows for them in the den, while we're gone," Evie says with a nod of her head.

I crouch into the snow next to the last working panel—praying it still works—and begin to brush off the snow. "We're not staying here."

The sun glints off one of the dark glass panels as I wipe the snow away. The sparkling flakes cling to my gloves, and I don't turn to look at Evie. I can picture the look on her face, the sympathy there at my delusions that we'll be rescued from this planet.

"Lisa..." she starts, the tone matching the picture in my head. I snap my head to look up at her over my shoulder.

"We're going back to Gragon 6," I say firmly. "We'll send a message using the escape pod. Or tinker with enough of the scraps left behind that we'll make something useable."

Evie frowns. "I'm not going to stop you, but—"

"You think we want to stay here?" I interrupt, gesturing towards the plains of white. The purple mountains silhouette in the distance, boxing us in on all sides. "Melanie didn't even want to step outside of the den. You think she wants to stay in rock caves, when she could be back on that luxurious moon of hers? Or Raegan? Finally free from the fighting pits, only to crash land here? This is not our end game, Evie. You may have found yourself a consolation prize and chosen to join the pack and stay, but it's not a fate I choose to accept. Not when there's still a chance to go home."

The cold wind whips between us as Evie purses her lips. My heart beats steadily, the adrenaline of my thoughts powering through me. I think I glimpse the outline of a teal figure near the edge of the ship. I turn away from Evie and furiously wipe the rest of the snow off the damn panel. A light next to it starts to blink, the sun's rays hitting it full force.

After what feels like a lifetime, Evie speaks. "This situation isn't ideal. Don't think because I've... I've found something here that means I don't miss Earth. Terra. That the idea of being surrounded by snow for the rest of my life brings a smile to my face. But sometimes... I think things happen for a reason. Whether we like them to—"

"You have *no idea* what we've been through," I spit, my anger ripping through me like venom. "You were asleep when you were taken, right? We weren't. We were finishing a job, doing what we loved, when they came for us."

Evie is quiet again. She looks away from me and says quietly, "Sometimes you need to weather the storm before you see the rainbow."

Chunhua's neck snaps and all I see is red as the words rip from my mouth. "Bull*fucking*shit. Don't try to tell me that two of my crew died just so I could find happily ever after in the arms of some wolf-shifting alien, on an uncharted wasteland. There's no rainbow here. And I'm not going to risk the lives of the others searching for one."

Evie visibly recoils, her eyes snapping back to mine. Before she can say any more, apologize or even try to push me to see the silver lining in any of the horror that has happened here, I push past her and hastily climb back down the ladder.

Juk is there, ready to help me down with those large warm hands of his. But my own words reverberate through me, and I jump down the last few broken rungs, ignoring his outstretched helping hands.

JUK

Something transpired on the *sheep's* roof between the alpha's mate and Leesa, and the tension between them carries throughout the day. I did not catch all that was spoken between them, their words too fast and sharp. Leesa's face was angry when she descended from the roof, and she stormed back into the *sheep* to assist Kay-tee with readying the language beam.

It is not my place to pry into matters that do not concern me, but an ache in my chest squeezes every time I see Leesa and her unhappy face. Something dark and angry clouds her—something that sets my intuition on edge. I want to ask what ails her, how I can help to make it right and wash the unease from her. But from the glare she gives me, I keep my distance.

It is not long before there is enough energy from the sunlight to fuel the language beam. Tabros is nervous to receive the beam, but excited. He is fidgety as the spindly spear points at him, and Leesa snaps at him to stay still. My stomach clenches at her anger. It is different than the roiling darkness that stinks around the sullen one left at the den.

"How bad is it?" Tabros asks, glancing over at me as Kay-tee presses small knobs on the strange rock in front of her. Lights blink on the reflective wall in front.

I pat Tabros on the shoulder firmly. My intuition tells me nothing will go wrong for him or Hazen. "No worse than getting scraped by a drackyr's claw. It will be over before you know it."

Moments later, the spear fires into Tabros's head and he collapses on the ground. Hazen tenses behind me, but I give him a reassuring nod. The quiet Celetan watches, waiting for Tabros to awaken. He does so a minute later, groaning as he sits up.

"I do not remember a drackyr leaving such a headache," Tabros winces as he rubs the side of his head.

"Then you have never fallen into a nest of them and had them all squawk at you at once," Hazen murmurs. Tabros laughs, and Kay-tee glances between the two of them, Hazen's words lost as he cannot yet speak Teeran. His eyes flicker to her briefly before he takes the spot before the spear, Tabros moving out of the way.

With a quick zap to the head, Hazen takes the language beam and falls to the floor.

Later in the evening, we settle by a fire outside. Tabros and Hazen have both recovered from the language transfer, and amuse themselves by testing out the Teeran words. Kay-tee smiles as Tabros tells a joke, and Hazen quietly offers her some charred meat.

"How come you like it burnt so?" Tabros asks. He is fascinated by the hoo-mans and their strange ways.

"Our stomachs digest it better when it is cooked," Ee-vee explains. She sits next to the alpha, an obvious distance between her and Leesa. Leesa sits quietly next to Kay-tee across the fire. I long to sit with her, but she has purposely distanced herself from the Celetans. Kay-tee sits closer, Hazen only an arm's length away, while the rest of us sit on the other side of the fire.

"Tastes better too," Kay-tee says quietly. "The idea of raw meat is unnerving to most humans."

"We shall smoke the rest and add it to our travel rations," the alpha says, as he nods to the leope carcass next to Baz.

"Tomorrow will be the first of long days of travel. Let us get a good rest tonight."

The conversation around the fire grows quiet as we finish our meal. I steal glances over at Leesa every few moments, but she stares into the fire, her thoughts far away. I want to know what occurred between her and the alpha's mate to cause such tension. Kay-tee is quiet too. She glances at Leesa, but does not speak to her.

Once the meal is done, Leesa and Kay-tee retire inside the sheep. Ee-vee chooses to sleep outside with the rest of us, curled up next to the alpha in his celestial form by the fire. Further indication there has been a rift between her and the other females. A rift between their two packs.

Hazen and Tabros take the first shift for watch, Tabros in celestial and Hazen in ancestral form.

And while I attempt to get sleep before it is time to switch off guard, I find all I can think about is Leesa and the pull Vekao has given me towards her.

Both moons are bright this night, the dark of clouds off in the distance. Tomorrow they shall cloud Vekao and Jaci's light, but not this night. My intuition tingles every so lightly with something. But whether it has to do with my mate and her reluctance to be with the pack or as an omen towards our journey to save the rest of her people, I do not know.

LISA

DAY 10

Most of the night, I am restless. While Katie sleeps soundly huddled against one wall, her spot from before we were rescued by the pack, I toss and turn.

Before too long, the moons are waning and I am up long before the sun. Katie is asleep, or at least pretends to be while I quietly strip the rest of the ship.

I don't know what I'm grabbing but I take as much as I can. Small chips and pieces of metal that could be useful. Somewhere there must be a piece of value, something that will help us be rescued from this frozen wilderness. Something to help us get back to Gragon 6.

I'm positive between the wreckage here and Briley's pod, we'll be able to put something together. I grip the thought tightly, needing the hope it brings more than I breathe air.

There's a tentative knock on the door. I look over my shoulder, black strands falling into my face before I push them back. I expect to see Juk, my heart leaping momentarily at the thought, but instead it's Evie. I ignore the disappointment that quietly hits my stomach, and file it away with the rest of the grief and tumble of emotions I plan to deal with later.

"We'll be leaving in about thirty minutes," Evie says. No good-morning, no other form of greeting. Not that I would have given her one in return. "I hope you two are ready for a long day of travel."

"We are."

I spin back around to find Katie awake and sitting up right. She smiles at Evie and nods her head.

"There's some tea on the fire right now, and some travel rations," Evie says directly to Katie this time.

Katie nods her thanks, and then Evie leaves. I look back over at her, watching as she murmurs something to the alpha and they both glance my way. Juk appears next to them and the three wander off to prepare the sleds, presumably.

"Don't give her the cold shoulder, Lisa," Katie suddenly says quietly.

I sigh and continue to strip the circuit in front of me. I've left the main motherboard intact, in case we need to take parts from the pod back here and use this for communication. "I'm not."

Katie scoffs and stands. I glance up at her as she places her hands on her hips. Without her black miner's outfit, she looks like she belongs in the pack. Covered in leather leggings and furs, she has the same warrior princess vibe as Evie. Something pangs in me, but I won't label it as jealousy. Her suit was ruined. There was no other option for her.

"What are you going to do if we're stuck here, Lisa?" she asks. Katie is normally quiet. Allison has always had enough gumption for both of them, enough spice to overpower them both. But Katie keeps to herself. She is quiet and observant, and that makes her the wiser of the twins more often than not.

"We're getting off this planet," I give as an answer. Circuit stripped, I shove the small metal pieces into my bag, careful not to crack any. With any luck, Katie will know how to put something together, or maybe we'll find out Meg is still alive...

"Lisa," she says with that tone that tells me I'm not about to like what she has to say, "you know the odds are not in our favour. This planet is uncharted."

"You've mentioned that a few times," I say.

"What Evie does with her life is up to her, not you," she says softly. "Is it really so bad she's happened to find happiness in this dire situation?"

"In seven days? Yes, a little," I snap. "Things don't happen that quickly in real life. This isn't a fairytale. For all we know, one of the astrostingents you scanned in the air is an aphrodisiac and none of what she feels is real."

A heartbeat passes between us before she says quietly, "And is that so bad?"

I groan as I finally meet her eyes. They're bright in the soft sunlight that comes through the cracked windshield. The rising sun's rays streak across her face, like a divine sign.

"Don't tell me you're falling for one of them too."

"Would that really be so bad?" she whispers. She then smirks, trying to lighten the tone. "You can't deny that they're not bad to look at."

I just scoff again, ignoring the increase in my heartbeat as an image of teal skin and muscles flashes before my eyes.

"Staying isn't an option," I say. "We're going to find the others and get off here, just you wait."

"And what if we don't? What if they're dead, Lisa?" Something in her throat catches as she says the words. Katie isn't often without Allison, and I know this is eating her up inside. "Or what if they're with that enemy pack they mentioned?"

"And what of our families back at home?" I snap. "Are you telling me you can so easily give them up, not fight to get back to them simply because we've stumbled across some attractive, primitive aliens?"

Katie is quiet. There is another knock on the doorway and my shoulders tense. Katie looks over my shoulder and then averts her eyes from the knocker.

It's Hazen. "I have come to collect your sleeping furs to put them back in the sled," he says in a quiet, deep voice. While Juk is normally reserved, Hazen is quiet. I don't know why I make the comparison, only that it comes fleetingly.

"We'll roll them up and bring them in a moment," I say dismissively. Hazen nods at me and glances over at Katie before returning outside. I spot the others around the fire, half in human form, half as wolves. I don't spot Juk.

"All of my family is here on this planet," Katie says in that quiet tone again. There's a somberness to it this time. "There is nothing for me to go back to on Gragon 6."

I make no comment at that. My siblings and I are not close. Most do not live on Gragon 6 anymore. I was the only one to withhold the family trade, to not break tradition. It made my grandfather proud, but he is about the only one left. And on his last legs at that. I don't remember the last time I visited him.

"People go missing in across the galaxy all the time, Lisa," she continues. "Whether they're taken or get lost.. It's a vast universe with many unknowns. But what I do know is that we happened to fall into friendly quarters. We've found a people who are not only willing to help us, but willing to accept us into their folds. I'd call that pretty lucky."

"Then you can cuddle up to one of them like Evie and stay here," I say. "But I'm going back home."

Katie groans in frustration. It's uncommon for her to argue with me, but I guess on this planet, everybody argues against me.

"Why, Lisa," she says, her voice rising as she waves her arms around her, "why is staying here such a terrible thing?"

"Because it means failure!" I shout. My heart rattles in my chest as the air catches in my lungs. Chunhua's neck snaps somewhere, and Delphine screams for help. "I failed Delphine and Chunhua, I'm not failing the rest of you!"

My legs feel like they're about to buckle, but I refuse to let them. Katie steps towards me, placing her hand on my shoulder.

"It's not your fault, Lisa," she says. Tears brim in her eyes, but she holds them in. "You can't fix what others have broken. None of this is your fault. Our lives were interrupted, taken from us. But none of it is your fault."

"Of course it is," I say. "I'm the foreman. I'm the leader of our crew. If I hadn't insisted on staying to finish that load—"

Katie cuts me off. "None of us would leave a score that big behind. It was an amazing find, and we'd have been foolish to leave it for another crew to finish excavating. It was just... bad luck."

"I should have been more careful," I continue, her words falling into the cracks of my reason, feeding my guilt instead.

"More protocols in check. I thought being the only female crew was something to celebrate, but... but I didn't think about how dangerous it would be. How vulnerable we'd be to a situation like this."

"Lisa," she says as she grips my shoulder. More sunlight starts to filter into the room, and I hear the bones snap as one of the Celetans outside shifts. "We don't know for certain the Skulchers were targeting women. It would have just been a coincidence. Maybe they were grabbing whatever humans they could. Maybe not. But we'll never know. And dwelling on it now won't help us rescue the others. Won't help us move on to the next steps of our life."

"But I'm your leader," I whisper, almost in defeat. The guilt and grief I hold pushes hard against Katie's words, against the rationale she is trying to instill in me. It tries to wash away the darkness of guilt, and bring light to the situation. But I can't let it.

"That was on Gragon 6," she says softly. "Here, you're just another lost human, wanting to survive. We're all in this together. Including Evie."

With one more squeeze on my shoulder, she turns back around and starts to roll up her blankets. I grip the strap of my bag, the fragments of chips and computer inside. Her words ring true, but I can't let go of the failure that haunts me. I can't let more of them die at my hands.

The day is long and cold. The Celetans run for hours on end, only stopping when absolute necessary. We stop only twice, once for lunch and once to relieve ourselves again, before we find a campsite for the night.

Axyll has planned the route based on how many shelters we can hit. It's clear once we approach the first shelter for the night, everyone is exhausted. My legs and back are cramped and stiff from sitting so long in the sled. Evie rode with us for most of the day, the alpha out at the front of the pack.

My spine cracks as I stand. The sound is thankfully brief enough that the haunting of Chunhua's death leaves me alone for once.

We climb out of the sled ourselves as the Celetans go shift. Tabros, Baz, and Kalpa stay in their wolf form. They run off to find something fresh to eat.

Evie gets the fire going outside of the cave. Katie helps her while I find fresh snow to boil for water.

Axyll is unsurprisingly the first to return in human form. He is the fastest at shifting, but Juk is not long behind him. My heart stutters at the sight of him, his towering height, and bright teal skin. He sweeps his hair back up into a bun on his head, and I turn back to getting the water boiling.

The green leather bag I have packed with snow keeps twisting above the fire. I try to steady it, but it refuses to cooperate.

"Let me help you," Juk's voice says from behind me. His hand nearly grazes the side of my head as he reaches out to adjust the water pouch. His arm is corded with muscle. The sight of it makes my insides burn with a longing I haven't felt in a long time.

Juk finishes adjusting the bag, where it sits perfectly above the fire now, and he then retreats to go ensure the inside of the cave is empty.

I watch after him, bewildered at the feelings I am fighting at bay. There are plenty of well-muscled men and women on Gragon 6, some of whom I have had the pleasure of spending the night with, but none of them have ever made me feel this way. *The astrostingents in the air must be making me feel this way* I think. *There's no way it's natural. Not this fast. Not without knowing him at all.*

JUK

The meal is a quiet one. Everyone is exhausted from our long journey here. My maw aches from pulling the females from hours on end. The sled is light, even with them in there, but the friction and movement of having the pulley in my mouth for so long makes it uncomfortable.

This particular shelter we are at is a small one. The females have built the fire near the entrance, close enough to bring warmth to the small interior, but not so close as to trap anyone inside, should there be an emergency.

Leesa and Kay-tee sleep inside the cave, while Ee-vee sleeps with her mate.

Clouds cover all of Jaci this night, and much of Vekao. She is still quite round, but each night shrinks smaller. Soon it will be a dark night, when her light does not shine at all, and then she will bless us with her presence once more.

At some point, deep in the dead of night a small sound wakes me from my sleep. There are whimpers coming from within the shelter. The smell of fear permeates the air, and I sit upright and alert.

"One of the females sleeps badly," Hazen says quietly. He is on watch in his ancestral form.

A small figure crawls out of the shelter from the other side of the fire. At once I know it is Leesa. She exits the cave without looking at us and walks out into the snow away from the fire. My Seeker watches as she goes, blinded by the sight of her. It never blinks, seeing all that is around us.

Hazen stands to follow her, but I grunt at him. He nods in response, understanding my meaning even though I am in celestial form and cannot speak.

I quickly stretch my legs, and dash around the opposite way that Leesa has gone. I shift quickly back into my ancestral form, throwing on a breechcloth and pulling up my hair before I stride toward her.

Leesa sits just around the corner from the shelter. The faint light from the fire reflects across her back, shadowing her against the hidden light from the moons.

She does not turn as I come towards her, my feet crunching in the snow. I sit close to her, but not so close as to encroach on her space. She hugs her knees, her eyes turned towards the clouds covering the moons, but as I sit next to her, she straightens and hastily wipes away the tears coming from her dark eyes.

My Seeker is blinded by her sadness. Her fear. I want to help, want to make it disappear. But it cannot sense the danger that she feels, cannot detect where the threat to her is coming from. And so, I sit quietly, giving her company.

Leesa shivers as another breeze rips through the air. The clouds move quickly above us, Vekao shining brightly for a moment before she is hidden again.

"It is warmer by the fire," I say quietly, unable to stay silent any longer. My arms itch to reach out and pull her closer, pull her into my embrace to shelter her from the cold.

"I'm fine," she says, her voice barely more than a whisper. It is a lie, for she shivers again. I start to reach out but stop when she rubs her hands up and down her arms, and I run my hand through my hair instead.

"You do not seem fine."

Leesa's eyes shift to me before she turns back to the covered moons. Her hands start to slow against her arms, and she lets out a long sigh. "It has been a rough week."

Week is a new concept for me, as my mind translates the words into days. Interesting. I stay quiet, hoping she will elaborate, but when she doesn't, I gently prod. "You were whimpering in your sleep."

Her eyes turn wide as she looks back at me. Sleek black strands of hair slide across her face in the wind, and I cannot help myself. I reach out and tuck the wayward strands behind her ear. My hearts pound wildly as her eyes meet mine. They are dark and glossy with tears, the brief glimpses of moonlight reflecting brightly in them.

"You.. you heard that?" she whispers.

I nod, dropping my hand. "Celetans have excellent hearing, especially when in our celestial form."

Leesa tilts her head. "'Celestial form'? Is that your wolf form?"

The word *wolf* brings up an image of a creature I have never seen before. I can see the comparison, however, though it looks to be closer to the size of a lupen than a Celetan. I nod my head.

"I've never met a shifting species before," Leesa continues. "There are many different species that make up the Gragon colonies, but none of them are shifters."

"Gragon... this is where you are from?" I ask. The image that comes up is nothing but a cluster of sparkling stars around a bright orb. *Is that what our home looks like, out there among the stars? Small and infinite against the greatness of Vekao and Jaci?*

Leesa nods. I spy the briefest of smiles on her face, before it disappears. "Yes. There are 8 Gragon colonies—8 different worlds, if you will. I am from Gragon 6. We are a mining colony. We dig for gems and minerals in the surrounding asteroids, and sell them within the colonies or to different planets. It's how we make our living."

I nod along, though do not really understand all of the images that come to my mind as it translates her words. It is hard for me to picture any other world than the one I am used to.

I look around at the snow, sparkling under the moonlight. I know these hills and mountains, this terrain as well as I know my own two tails. It is all I have ever known, and the idea of being thrust into a different world, as Leesa says, is difficult to imagine. It makes my intuition hum with danger, and I can only imagine what it must be like for her and her people to come here.

"Is it very different than here?"

Leesa nods. "Very. There is no snow on Gragon 6. It never snows."

"Snow is new to you then?"

She shakes her head. "No. Gragon 8 is covered in snow most of the year. They export ice and Frost Gems."

We fall in silence once more. I am used to silence. I do not mind it usually, and prefer to save my words for when they count. But this silence between Leesa and I makes me uneasy. I want to hear her speak. I want to lift the weight of her troubles off her shoulders. For once in my life, I do not like the silence that has fallen.

I think of her whimpering in her sleep. Of the tears she has dried away and of the slump in her shoulders as she rests her arms on her knees.

My mouth opens to speak, to fill the void with finding answers to what plagues her, but she speaks first.

"Tell me about Vekao."

I blink in surprise. My Seeker shines, and as though she heard her name, Vekao appears from behind the clouds. Her bright blue light bathes us. It washes over everything as her large round curve comes into view, sparkling the snow around us. It shines off Leesa's glossy black hair and is reflective in her dark eyes as she turns to look at me. The clouds keep Jaci hidden, knowing this moment is for Vekao.

"Vekao..." I do not know where to start. How to describe something so magnificent, something so meaningful, so essential to our way of life...

"She is a granter of gifts. She guides us and watches over our pack," I say slowly.

"Gifts? What gifts?" Leesa asks, the skepticism not lost in her voice.

I tap the light blue crystal imbedded in my forehead—my Seeker. "She grants us our celestial form. Vekao is all knowing and blesses those under her guidance."

"She gave you your crystal—your Seeker?" she asks.

I nod. "Everyone is born with a Seeker, for everyone is blessed at birth by Vekao. Some say our ancestors used to only turn under the light of her full moon. Eventually, she granted us with the power to turn whenever we needed."

Leesa looks thoughtfully up at Vekao. I do not know if I am explaining the importance of her enough, that I can truly convey what the great moon means to the pack. I wonder if her people had their own version of Vekao—or perhaps, more worryingly, if they are like the Stygians and do not follow suit.

It does not matter what she believes or did on her Gragon 6, I remind myself, *Vekao has brought her and her people here for a reason. She deems them as worthy, even if they do not worship her as Celetans do.*

"And what of the smaller moon?" she asks.

"That is Jaci," I say, feeling like I am teaching one of the young cubs. "Some say she is the ward of Vekao. Some say they lost a great battle for dominance. The Ashen Pack follows her guidance."

"And what does your pack think of her?"

I tilt my head in thought. I can see the small outline of Jaci through the clouds, the yellow light in contrast to Vekao's bright blue.

"I cannot speak for the pack, but Jaci means little," I say finally. "She is a helper to Vekao, perhaps at times, but otherwise, little more than just a moon. Just as the stars are nothing but decoration in Vekao's mighty sky."

"And the other pack—the one where the women might be—they worship the stars?" Leesa asks carefully.

"Yes." My fists curl at the thought of the Stygians, but I try to keep relaxed. "They are an affront to Vekao with their lack of respect."

"But you just said the Ashen tribe worship the smaller moon," Leesa says. "Are they not an affront as well?"

"The Ashen Pack should not exist," is all I say.

Leea leans back on her arms as she looks up at both moons. For a brief moment, both of their light pierces through the clouds, before a strong gust comes along and blankets us both back into near darkness.

"And what about us? Are we expected to worship a moon now that you've taken us into your pack?" Leesa asks. "Or are we an affront to nature as well?"

There is a bite to her words. A bitterness as she turns to look at me, her eyes narrowing. It pierces through my soul, my Seeker shining with worry as my intuition blazes with Leesa's anger. She does not want to be here.

"You are not Celetan," I say. "Even if you do not worship Vekao, she has brought you here for a reason. And that is good enough for me."

This is not what Leesa wants to hear. She jumps up suddenly, anger blazing in her eyes. I never get to ask her what ails her, what causes her to whimper in her sleep, for she comes right up to my face and sneers. Even in her anger, she is beautiful. Her dark eyes and lightly tanned skin make my hearts sing, even if her words twist my stomach.

"Nothing about coming here is good."

JUK

DAY 11

The next morning my hearts feel heavy. Leesa's angry words echo in my head throughout the night, and sleep eludes me. I take Tabros's guard shift since I am awake anyway.

By the time the sun rises, the clouds are thick and cover the sky in a dark grey shroud. The sun is nowhere to be seen as the wind whips through our encampment. The fire flickers endlessly, threatening to blow out with every gust that comes through.

Its flickering flame wavers uncertainly, much like my intuition. Something gnaws at it, twisting with unease in my stomach. It makes my shoulders tense and my senses alert.

Nothing feels off in the scent of the wind, but something is coming. Something I cannot see.

"Juk."

I turn away from the sled I am packing, securing the rescue items within. Kalpa is careless with his pulling, jostling the supplies around while he runs. It is nothing to fuss over, but I find my hands need to be kept busy to keep my mind clear.

My alpha comes towards me. His white hair flickers in the wind, whipping around his face as the gusts grow angrier. "Are you alright? Tabros says you did not sleep."

"I am fine, alpha," I say. Axyll's eyes narrow at me, his Seeker's ability able to see my unease clouding my aura. "Something does not feel right, but I cannot place what it is."

"The storm perhaps?" Axyll asks as he gestures to the growing winds around us. Small flurries of snow start to fall, and the nip in the air picks up. It will be cold for the females on this day, colder than the one before. We will need to move swiftly.

My lips purse into a thin line. It could be the storm, that is true. "Perhaps. It is unclear to me. I do not like it."

Axyll nods and claps a hand on my shoulder. "It will not make for a good day of travel, that is for sure. The females will be frozen in the sled. We'd better start our journey now, before the snowflakes grow fatter."

We are fast to pack up the camp and females, and start our journey. Our next planned stop is quite far away. With good weather, we would get there just after sunset. But in this weather, I fear we will not even make it halfway.

The pack moves as fast as possible. Wind whips through my fur, pushing it in every direction as the icy flakes stick to each end. The cold bites through to the skin, something that is rare for a Celetan.

I glance back at the females huddled in the large sled. They are nothing but blurs through the white whirl of the storm. The sled is right behind me, and yet it takes my Seeker to ensure that they are alright, as my eyes struggle to see through the snow. It pierces through the blinding wind and makes note of each female. The three of them are huddled together. Snow and ice cling to them as it does our fur, but they are not in distress. Not yet.

We press on a bit longer. It is not until it is just past noon that Axyll lets out a howl, the signal that we must find shelter. We will not make it to our planned destination today, not in this storm. The flurries are so thick now I can barely make out the alpha in front of me.

Tabros runs up to Axyll, and the two shortly converse. It's a series of growls and snarls that I barely hear over the wind, and then we're off.

Baz runs close to the sled by my side, likely checking on the females as we race through the wind. My nerves spike as my intuition incessantly tells me something is wrong—or will be—and for a moment, I worry for the females in the sled. Perhaps they were more frozen than I thought, than my Seeker could see.

Baz would stop us if something was wrong, I remind myself. And yet, I cannot help but picture the females back there, frozen as icicles.

Soon, I see where we are headed. There is a small hunter shelter tucked into one of the mountain's faces up ahead. However, it is tiny. One of the smallest caves we have claimed as a shelter for our pack. I wonder how we will all fit in there, what the alpha's plan is, but I understand it is the closest cave to us. The females will not last much longer in this storm.

Tabros is in his ancestral form by the time I arrive with the larger sled. Naked, as the supplies are with Kalpa next to me. He is quick to help the females out, and usher them into the cave.

I watch them carefully. They are frozen, moving with slow, stiff movements, and I can hear the chatter of their teeth over the wind. My eyes watch Leesa until she disappears into the shelter of the cave and out of the harsh wind.

Kalpa and I hesitate with the sleds. There is nowhere for us to store them safely. They will be buried under the snow by the time the storm passes. It is a matter for us to figure out in the morning, lest we be buried with them.

We shift quickly outside. I do not worry about Leesa hearing the snap of our bones, for the wind is so loud. The sound still bothers her and I wish I knew why. I hate that something so natural to us causes her discomfort.

Inside the cramped cave, Kalpa hands out loincloths to the waiting Celetans. Modesty, for the females' sake. Though they look too frozen to care or glance at our icy cocks.

The three of them are huddled together in one corner. Axyll murmurs angrily under his breath. He tries to build a fire, but it is useless. This cave is a so small, only meant for emergencies, such as this, but not for so many people. And it is meant to be used in our celestial form.

There is no firepit here. Tabros has grabbed some of the fuel starters we packed in the supply sled, and the two of them have made a small spot in the centre of the floor. But the wood is damp from the storm and will not stay alight.

"I-it won't k-k-k-keep?" Ee-vee asks Axyll as she breaks away from Leesa and Kay-tee.

Axyll shakes his head. "They are too damp from the storm, and there is a wind current that comes in from down that narrow path," the alpha says. He points to a small pit of blackness near the other end of the short cave, which leads into a narrow, darkened path that we do not use. It is too small. "It keeps extinguishing anything we get started."

Ee-vee's already pale face blanches. The scent of her fear permeates, and she glances towards the other two women. "What are we to do then?"

The alpha sighs and glances towards me. The wind screams against the main entrance behind me. It echoes inside, the sound like an angry spirit haunting the cave. I shiver, but not from the cold—from my intuition.

"What do you feel?" Axyll murmurs to me. Ee-vee watches us closely, leaning in to hear, but I shake my head.

"Same as before. I cannot say what."

Axyll looks back at his mate. He brings her into his arms and hugs her close. They squeeze close together, and she is buried by his height and the blue of his skin. A ripple of envy skitters under my skin as I glance towards Leesa and her small form. Her arm is around Kay-tee, who shakes violently from the cold.

"We will need to huddle together for warmth," the alpha says at last. He looks down at his mate, who meets his eyes. "This cave is meant for use in our celestial form. We will need to shift back if we wish for any sort of warmth. The weather is too dangerous to move to the next cave."

"So..." Ee-vee starts. She looks over at the other two hoo-mans again.

"They can choose who they wish to huddle with," Axyll says at last. "They will be warmest that way. The other two Celetans will crowd the entrance to block out the wind."

Ee-vee chews on her lip and nods. "I'll tell the others."

Axyll nods. He presses his lips to her head, and again, that need, that longing runs through me. Not to press my lips against Ee-vee's brown hair, but to black, silky strands instead. "We will bring in some rations for you to eat. Then we will need to hunker down until the storm passes, or until morning. Whichever comes first."

I watch Ee-vee's movements as she walks over to the other two females. Their heads huddle close together as she explains the situation to them. Suddenly Leesa's head snaps up and her eyes meet mine. I hold my breath as an unreadable expression crosses her face. Kay-tee surveys the other Celetans, but her eyes linger on Hazen.

Soon the alpha's mate comes back to us. Axyll still tries to light a fire, but it is fruitless. He pauses his efforts as she relays the decisions back to him.

"Katie will huddle with Hazen, and Lisa with Juk," she says.

My hearts start to race. They beat out of control as every part of me itches to turn and look over at Leesa. But I fight it. I will not show how it excites me. Not when she is not welcoming yet of our union. Not when she does not understand we are meant to be mates. Not when she spits angry words at me that nothing good has come from being here.

"It is decided then," Axyll says. "We will go and shift. Tabros will bring you some rations before shifting himself."

Without another word, I rush back out into the storm and shift the fastest I have ever done.

LISA

I thought I'd felt cold before. Once back home, when we were stuck in a shaft well below the allotted limit, before Chelsea came on board as our Holder, and one of our beams broke due to a code malfunction. It was nearly seventeen hours before we were dug out from that pit. No sunlight, nothing but pitch black as we waited and shivered, Delphine praying quietly the whole time for our rescue.

With a glance over to Katie beside me, I know she's thinking the same thing: this is worse than that. While the seven of us had huddled together that night, holding one another through the endless darkness and the shaking from the cavern threatening to collapse on us completely, we were no near as cold as we are now.

My teeth cannot stop chattering. It is impossible. Icicles coat my eyelashes and drip from my nose, despite that it is covered over three times with a scarf-like fur that wraps around my face. Any bit of skin exposed feels raw and sore, bitten to death by the raw bite of the unforgiving cold.

Katie shakes uncontrollably beside me. Her eyes don't leave the alpha's fruitless attempts to light a fire. No matter how hard he tries, the flames will not stay. And when I see Kalpa shiver from the cold? That's when I know it is dire.

So, when Evie tells me there's a way to keep warm, hope floods me. We won't freeze here tonight. We'll make it through this storm, find the others, and I'll be the leader my crew deserves. I won't fail them as I failed Chunhua and Delphine.

But then she tells us *how* we will keep warm. And my heart stops. From anticipation or dread, I'm unsure. I swallow thickly before answering, trying to make it seem as though I *need* to think about my options before I decide on Juk. But in honesty, his name is instantly on the tip of my tongue. I nearly breathe it out, and that alone, scares me.

I am not staying on this planet. Regardless of what may be building inside me.

Minutes tick by, the longest of my life. Longer than when Chunhua's neck snapped and the Skulchers took us onto their ship. Longer than the ship breaking apart and crashing into the snow.

Soon through the howling winds that scream at the entrance to the cave, three large forms appear. The largest one catches my eye immediately, and my stomach flips.

I hold my breath, my body still shaking from cold, as two of the large wolves approach us. It is easy to discern Hazen from Juk. While still frightening and large, his size is nothing compared to Juk. Even the alpha looks small compared to the giant wolf that looks as though he could eat me whole with one snap of his jaws.

Hazen huffs something at Katie, his disturbing third eye never leaving her face. He shepherds her towards the end of the cave. There, he circles a moment before settling into the ground against a seam in the rock that looks like a narrow path.

Katie does not hesitate to lie down against him. He lays his two tails over her like a blanket, and she nestles in close, too cold to be shy. I must do the same.

Juk is taller than me, even as a wolf. The bottom of his muzzle meets my forehead as I look up at him. He stares down his nose at me, his Seeker looking at me over the end of his snout. It sends a shiver over my body, as though it can see through me. Like it can see my secrets, see the grief that has taken over my heart, the fear that runs through my veins, and see the blush that tries to creep down my chest if it wasn't so cold. Like it knows how I feel and what I am trying to fight.

Juk herds me over closer to where Hazen and Katie lay. Already with the two of them settled, the cave feels cramped. I don't know how we expect to fit another couple in here.. and then there is still Kalpa and Baz.

I settle down on the ground near Katie, and wait for Juk to join me. He fumbles a bit with his size, trying to configure himself in a way that leaves enough space for his alpha and Evie.

Once he is settled on the ground, I try to be bold like Katie. But I hesitate. I know this is necessary, but it feels like a line that once crossed, I can't move back. *Am I really debating between huddling with a guy or freezing to death?*

White fur greets me as I hold my breath and nestle next to him. The snow sticking to the white strands is melting. Which means, despite how I feel, it is warmer in here than out there.

Juk shifts slightly, and I nestle closer. Before I can think, I rub my face into the fur, the droplets from the melting ice running on my face. I can feel the warmth radiating from his enormous body. It bellows out with each of his breaths, and there, beneath the fur and flesh, I can hear the erratic sound of his hearts.

Somewhere, I recall, it was mentioned they have two hearts. Juk's beat rapidly. I chalk it up to a normal rate, refusing to think it might be because of me. Just because *my* heart rate may be elevated due to our forced proximity, doesn't mean his is the same. Doesn't mean this means anything more to him than survival.

Two large tails wrap themselves over me. They're incredibly soft, different than the thick wiry hairs springing from the rest of his body. Their heavy weight comforts me, grounding me to this moment as warmth ebbs back into my body, and my limbs stop shaking. My teeth stop chattering. Something heavy lifts off my shoulders, and it's not his tails, but the journey itself. The fear and purpose that drives me forward is quiet for a moment, replaced with the whipping of the wind outside, and the two heartbeats hammering in Juk's chest.

And as my eyes fall heavy, I find myself trying to make sense of the heartbeats, to see if there is a distinguishable pattern between the two, as I drift off into a deep, dead sleep.

JUK

DAY 12

The wind quiets sometime during the deep of night. The clouds migrate, and the bright light from the moons embraces the entrance of the cave. I watch as the shadows move, and slowly, the sky grows light as the sun breaks the horizon.

There was no sleep for me this night. Not while Leesa lay cuddled tight against me. Not with her scent putting my hearts into a frenzy, with the soft sound of her odd heartbeat keeping time with mine. She is so small and fragile next to me, like a newborn cub that I worry the slightest of my movements may hurt her.

Not that there is any room for me to move. We are nearly piled on one another in this small shelter. Hazen is pushed up against the back of the cave, covering the draft from the narrow tunnel hidden there. Kay-tee is barely seen buried beneath his tails.

We are next to them. My tails cover the front space between them and Leesa. At my back, I feel the press of a rock wall, and some of another warm body. My alpha, by the scent.

For most of the night, while the storm raged, Kalpa and Baz huddled together at the entrance. One would be outside, the other just inside the lip of the cave, and they would switch when the one outside was too cold. A restless night for them too.

With the storm past and dawn breaking, Kalpa and Baz leave the cave to hunt for food. Fresh meat is best for us in this form, and given that we had to abandon our journey so early yesterday...

My stomach rumbles at the thought, and I still, worrying it will wake Leesa. She stirs momentarily, but stays asleep. The hoo-mans are exhausted, the cold wearing them down quickly. I wonder what we can do to help keep them warmer.

Axyll grunts something behind me. A suggestion to wake and stretch our legs. Perhaps now we can get a small fire started for the females that will stay lit.

Someone near the front grunts in response. Baz, by the sound of the deep growl. He must have returned already with food. Soon I hear the snapping of bones, and I tense, hoping the sound does not wake Leesa. Next time we have a private moment together, I will ask her why the sound disturbs her so.

Moments later, the soft crackle of a fire sounds just outside the cave. The alpha moves behind me, and I hear Ee-vee murmur something to him, and he chuckles slightly, as much as one can in their celestial form.

Cold rushes into the spot where my back met up against the alpha as he leaves, but it gives me space to stretch a bit. A crick in my neck cracks, bringing relief to a tense spot I did not know was there.

The movement disturbs Leesa and she wakes. She stirs abruptly, her body stiff against mine. The sudden change causes my fur to stand on end. Fear leaks into her scent, and it strikes me in the hearts. My Seeker shines brightly all around the cave. It blinds me, and a growl loosens from my lips, beyond my control. Something is wrong.

Leesa relaxes. Whatever fear she felt dilutes, the ever-present anxiety the only thing there. She sits up, lightly pushing my tails aside, and they swish out of her way.

"Morning," she murmurs, her eyes briefly meeting mine, and a warmth spreads through me. I can't recall receiving a simple greeting from her before. It's private, only for me, and it makes my hearts sing.

Before I can stop myself, before I even think, my head leans forward and I lick her lightly across the cheek. The gesture is more natural than breathing air, and yet she stiffens at it. I freeze in realizing what I have done. My Seeker is still blinded by something, perhaps my own fear this time, my own embarrassment. Warning me of this misguided step, perhaps.

Leesa abruptly stands. She shakes off the melted snow from her suit, and glances behind her to where Hazen and Kay-tee have not moved.

I glance behind me. Hazen's eyes meet me, his Seeker closed. He blinks at me, and I snuff in response. Kay-tee is still asleep. Best to let her rest a little longer.

As Leesa moves to the front of the cave and the fire that awaits, I stretch out my legs as much as the small space allows me. My hearts still beat rapidly, my fur on end, and my Seeker blinding. The fear off Leesa is gone, and my own stupidity, my own forwardness should not cause such a response.

And yet, because of my actions, I do not feel it until it is too late. My intuition is momentarily clouded by my feelings for Leesa, for the move I have made that may have just jeopardized everything, as small as it may be.

It is only when the ground begins to tremor that I realize the heightened sense of danger is my intuition. My Seeker is blinded by the cave because of what is coming.

Everything begins to shake. I let out a roar, a warning growl that comes too late. Leesa whips behind me, her face wrought in confusion as I leap towards her. The rock ceiling begins to crumble, and cascades down on us as I tackle her out of the cave.

Outside, Ee-vee lets out a scream as she clings to Axyll's large form, while he lets out a loud howl. Another sharp whine pierces through the air, and it is not until the earth stops shaking that I realize it comes from me.

LISA

One minute, Juk is licking my cheek. It's affectionate, intimate, and my heart warms. That warmth spreads through my body, warmer than anything huddling next to his body gave me last night. This is a warmth from the *soul*, and yet I refuse to think more on it. He is here. My place is on Gragon 6. End of story.

But in the next moment, he lets out a growl. It shocks me, and for a disturbed moment, I think it's some territorial wolf-bullshit. Like he thinks I'm rebuffing his affection, when really I'd love nothing *more* than to give into these feelings, to find a bit of peace and happiness like Evie has found in this shitstorm of a situation—but I can't. Not when half of my crew is still missing, not when two deaths are still fresh in my conscience.

Soon my whole body is shaking in rage at the idea, but no. It's not my body shaking, but the *cave*. And then I realize the growl is meant for me, yes, but it is a warning. I can hear the crumbling of the rocks above me, shaking like bones, and my eyes go wide.

White fur flies at me, and I am thrown out of the cave. Juk's weight against me is like a rock thrown against a leaf, and I soar out into the snow. I knock into Evie, and we tumble into the snow next to Axyll. He lets out a loud, haunting howl as the cave entrance behind us collapses, and Juk lets out a piercing whine.

Next to me, Evie is shocked. She does not move as she stares at the rubble of rock. A blue blur rushes past me, and I run to their side.

One of Juk's tails is stuck beneath the rocks. The other one lashes wildly, desperate for its twin to be freed. Juke tries to twist his body to dig at the rocks, but he can't. It's a sight to behold, such a large, fearsome creature, held in place. Helpless and vulnerable. *Just like we were when the Skulchers took us.*

Baz starts to pull and throw rocks off the tail. I do the same. My arms ache with the effort of the first one, but I move on to the next. And then the next. Some of them are the size of my head.

Juk pulls his tail free. The fur is dirty and there is a kink at the end that was not there before. It hangs limp next to the other one. His eyes meet mine, his Seeker moving the fastest I have ever seen any of their third eyes move. It searches me for injuries, I realize.

My arm moves of its free will as I reach out to him, about to stroke his muzzle. It could have been so much worse. We could have been trapped or crushed.

Our eyes meet and then—we both realize. Dread plummets into my stomach, as I turn towards the rubble and start to scream.

"KATIE!"

Baz is still digging furiously at the rocks. Juk nudges him out of the way and tries to move them with his mouth. Paws. Anything. But it soon proves better in human form, and he starts to shift beside me.

I don't even hear the bones snapping. The white noise of my blood rushing in my ears is all I can hear. I don't need to hear them shift to picture Chunhua's snapped neck. Delphine's bloody back. It's all I can see as I blindly reach for rocks and throw them to one side, only for more and more to appear. The rough texture rips at my gloves.

Katie is all I have left. I never wanted to admit it. Never wanted to give into that pit of despair waiting to swallow me up if we can't find the others. Katie would be that light in that pit. We would grieve together. We would survive together. We would figure out our next steps together.

But now...

Juk is next to me, panting from his shift. Naked and stark teal against the white of the snow and grey rocks, he hauls the rocks aside with ease. Axyll is next to him now, also naked, and the three of them move the rocks as though they weigh nothing.

There are too many of them. We know it, but we don't stop. I don't know what Evie is doing. I don't care if she is still there, frozen still in shock. The rocks are endless, and the pit of grief threatens to swallow me whole.

Axyll suddenly lifts his hand and the Celetans immediately stop. I hesitate, a rock in my hand. The three of them tilt their heads to the rubble in unison, and then slowly, delayed, I hear it. Muffled voices.

"Katie!" I shout into the rocks. I can't discern the voice. I can't hear what they are saying.

I scramble up the rocks, trying to find a better place to hear them. I press my ear against the frozen stone, but it does not help.

A warm hand lands on my shoulder. Tears are frozen to my eyes, my chest frozen with hope. I dare not breathe as I look up at Juk. His eyes meet mine, his chest still heaving from his efforts. The gem in his forehead sparkles, shining just for me.

I step aside as Juk takes my place. He presses his ear where mine once was, and shouts into the rocks.

"Hazen!" he says. The rest is lost to his native tongue. I hear a muffled response, barely a whisper through the rocks, but Juk nods his head.

Axyll joins us, gently moving Juk to the side. He presses his ear to the spot, and nods his head as well, before yelling back in their Celetan language.

"What is happening?" I ask. My stomach is in knots, and my mouth feels dry. "Is... is Katie ok?"

Juk lifts a finger to my lips, silencing me. He tilts his head towards the rock, where the muffled shouting continues. *Can he hear them from here? Is his hearing that much better?*

Axyll nods and yells something back once more before standing. He turns to me with an unreadable expression, and glances towards Juk before speaking. Evie and the other Celetans stand at the bottom of the rock pile, waiting.

The alpha clears his throat, and I hold my breath.

"They are alive," he says with a breath of relief. The air *whooshes* out of me, and tears I didn't know I was holding in start to spill down my cheeks. I wipe them away before they can freeze, and Juk squeezes my shoulder.

"Oh, thank God," Evie says.

"There are too many large boulders to move from this spot. They have tried on their end, but it is too tight," Axyll continues. He pauses for a moment, glancing at me, before looking back over everyone else. I brace myself. I know that look. He is about to tell me something I do not want to hear. "We are to continue on our mission to find the others—"

He was right to pause. Immediately I open my mouth to argue, but Axyll talks over me, my anger ignored.

"Hazen and Kay-tee will make their way through the narrow back entrance, and head through the caves," he says over me.

"Why don't we wait for them on the other side?" I ask. "I'm not leaving Katie behind."

Juk gently squeezes my shoulder again. "It is a two-day walk to the other side," he says softly. I wrench my shoulder out from under his large, warm palm, and turn my angry stare up to him. "We will lose time reaching the others if we try to catch up to Hazen and Kay-tee. It is a maze of caves for them to navigate to the exit—but it is safe. Hazen knows his way through the caves, and once they are out, they will make their way back to the den."

My gut twists. My heart wrenches. My blood boils. I do not like any of this. The idea of leaving behind one of my crew makes my stomach sick. Katie is soft and quiet, nervous enough from being separated from her twin. But to be separated from everyone completely? To be stuck in the company of a stranger?

I turn away from Juk and realize that everyone is looking at me. Waiting for me to argue, to explode, to fight back against their Alpha's command. My fists curl at my sides, and I look back at the mountain of rock. At the boulders beneath my feet, at the pile we've already moved aside that made barely a dent in the heap of rubble.

My knees slam down onto the rocks as I face them once more. "Katie!" I shout.

I hear a muffle, female sound from within the rocks. I can't hear what she's saying, and more tears run down my cheeks. I feel like I can barely catch a breath as I push on to say the words that make me want to throw up.

"W-We're moving on. To find the others," I shout. It turns into a sob. "We'll meet back at the den. When I see you again, I'll have the others. I promise. I won't let you down."

Katie's response is lost on me, buried behind the rubble, and drowned out by the sound of my sobs. Juk reaches out again, but I jerk out of reach. I avoid Evie's reach of comfort too, and trudge my way through the deep snow and back to the sleds.

"Come on then," I say, my words wobbling. "If there's nothing else we can do here, then let's go."

JUK

It is a solemn ride to our next camp. We make good progress, crossing over a vast distance, but the cave's collapse has devastated our spirit.

My tail is in a lot of pain. It limps to the side, dragging on the ground, and with every pull of the sled, pain courses through it. As a result, I move slower, running at a speed where my paws do not hit the ground as hard. It helps, but by the time we reach the shelter for the night, my tail is throbbing.

Our shelter is spacious. This is where we should have been the night before, had the storm not thrown us off course. Now, we must make up time, a luxury that was scarce to begin with.

It is a heavy feeling that hits us, as this unspoken thought hangs in the air. We finish securing the sleds as the females head inside the cave.

Leesa has not said a word since we left Kay-tee and Hazen behind. Not a word was uttered between her and Ee-vee as I pulled them in the sled, and now, she strides into the cave without even looking at the alpha's mate. Axyll murmurs something to his mate as the two of them head inside.

The glow from the fire greets me as I join the others after shifting into my ancestral form. Leesa sits on one side of the fire, away from the others, as Kalpa skins a fresh kill and the alpha burns the meat for the females.

While the others seem content in letting Leesa stew in her quiet anger alone, I will do no such thing. I move next to her side and sit in front of the fire. She may refute what I know to be true—that we are mates—because her mind is occupied with finding the others of her pack, of finding a way back into the stars, but I will look after her until then. This is what I have decided. Though she may fight the feeling between us, the destiny that my Seeker knows to be true, I will care for her as a mate would. As my hearts long to do. If she wishes to stew in silence and anger, I will stay by her side. Should she need a shoulder to weep on, mine will be there.

Tabros comes in from the cold and shakes his body as though he is still sporting fur. He sighs and turns to the Alpha.

"Kalpa is right—the smaller sled has been damaged."

I turn curiously to the others. This conversation must have started while I was shifting. "Damaged?"

Kalpa nods from where he plucks feathers off a second drackyr Baz brought in before running to hunt more food. "I noticed it while pulling. It keeps listing off to the right."

"Can it be fixed?" Axyll asks as he hands his mate a piece of charred meat. We will not eat until he has taken the first bite, but he will not eat until his mate does. Ee-vee glances at Leesa who has not yet been served, and I eye the meat charring on the rocks near the fire. I take the cue and find a piece for her. She takes it, but does not start eating, instead choosing to hold it and stare into the flames. *She will eat when she is ready.* I know her mind is on Kay-tee.

Tabros shakes his head. He is particularly handy and was a big instrument in the sleds' construction.

"Part of the frame is cracked. One rough jostle and it will snap," he says. He then grimaces as he glances towards Leesa and back to the alpha. "And some of the supplies have been damaged as well. A bag of smoked meat was ripped open, and is now frost bitten. It may be salvageable, but... I think we will need to abandon the sled for now and move the supplies into the other."

The alpha considers this as he takes a fresh piece of raw drackyr and throws it into his mouth. *Finally*, I think, my stomach grumbling as I reach out and pick up one of the raw pieces waiting to be consumed.

It is chewy and coppery, the taste of its sweet blood coating my tongue. I do not think I have eaten since yesterday morning before the storm set in, and my stomach rumbles happily in response. I reach for another piece when I notice Leesa looking at the raw meat with disgust. She glances towards me, but quickly dart away when she catches my eye.

I chuckle to myself, but make sure I turn my mouth away from her as I slip the next piece between my lips.

"I don't need to be in the sled," Ee-vee says, her mouth full of the charred meat. She swallows and turns to the alpha. "I can ride on your back."

Tabros considers this. "With one less in the sled, I think we should be able to fit the supplies in next to Leesa."

"I can ride on Juk, if need be."

I whip my head back to the right, eyes wide. Leesa continues to gaze into the flames, her food still untouched. Were her words imagined? Is my Seeker playing tricks on me, making me hear what my heart desires?

But the others turn their heads towards Leesa as well. It was not imagined then. My hearts sore, my pulse quickening at the thought of her riding on my back as Ee-vee does the alpha. I have never had someone ride on my back other than the pups or cubs for fun in the den.

"Then that is settled," Axyll says. He pulls his mate in close, wrapping his arm over her shoulder. She huddles closer, eating another piece of charred meat.

I glance back over to Leesa next to me. How would it feel to wrap my arm around her, tuck her small form next to mine? To have her nuzzle against me for warmth, to embrace her within my arms?

My hearts beat rapidly, but of course I do not move. Leesa stares into the fire, but at last starts to eat the meat. *Good.* Before she finishes, I take another of the cooked meat pieces and place it near her.

If I can't wrap my arms around her, the least I can do is take care of her in every other way possible.

LISA

I hate this cave. I hate the warm, secure fire that crackles at my back. I hate that Evie is curled next to Axyll, the two of them sharing a bundle of furs comfortably, sleeping in peace. I hate the soft snores emitting from Kalpa or Tabros.

I hate that we're *safe and sound* while Katie is in a maze of caves. No sunlight, no fire, nothing—or at least, that's how I picture it. Gods-knows what supplies or food or anything they're able to muster. I hate how I don't know if she's injured, or if Hazen is. If she's dependent on him and he's injured...

My eyes squeeze shut and I roll over to face the fire. The furs around me are tangled from tossing and turning. Sleep eludes me as guilt eats me from the inside out. *We should have gone to meet them. Should have traveled to where the tunnels lead out of the cave.*

But then my stomach twists again, dropping at an alarming speed as I think of the others. Of Allison, Chelsea, Gabby, and Vivianna. They need our rescue more than Katie. They still—presumably—don't know any form of safety on this planet yet, while we do. Katie is safe with Hazen, I know this. Melanie is safe back at the Snowscape's den, safe with the pack, with these people. And I'm...

Shifting ever so slightly, I tilt my head to look up across the fire. Juk dozes near the cave's entrance. He is in his human form, while Baz is in wolf form on the other side of the large opening.

Juk sits leaning against the wall, his head folded forward onto his chest, his arms crossed. I watch the casual rise and fall of his chest, even and deep, as he sleeps. I glance at Evie huddled with Axyll, their two forms molded into one. Evie's brown hair is barely discernable against the tall form of the alpha, with his light blue skin and stark white blonde hair.

What would it be like, to curl up against Juk? Against his solid body, his strong arms, and comforting touch. I close my eyes and think back to yesterday—to this morning. His fur was warm, the beating of his hearts soothing as the push of his large lungs in and out against me soothed me to sleep. Would it be similar snuggling up against him whilst in human form? To have those arms around me instead of fur, for our bodies fit together, like two pieces of a puzzle. Is it wrong that I feel so safe at that thought, while there are four of my crew lost in the wilderness of this planet, and Katie is traipsing through darkened caves?

Maybe she and Evie are right though, I think. Bad things happen no matter where we are. I never thought Gragon 6 was dangerous, outside of the mines, but that's where we were taken. From our own backyard.

There is no guarantee what tomorrow will bring. It will hopefully bring us closer to the others. And once we find them... what next?

I knew I was delusional in thinking we'd find a way off this planet. These people, while kind and generous, are centuries behind in technology. Millennia even. They are in a stone age, while we are in the space age. Unless there is any equipment from the cargo hold or Briley's pod that proves useful... we are stuck here. Possibly forever. And if I'm stuck here forever...

My eyes again find Evie and Axyll curled together. Twelve days. We'd been on this planet for twelve days now, and she, at least, had found a silver lining. Something to hold on to if the *forever here* is our end game.

Would it make me a bad leader if I found that too? If I took care of my people, my crew and my friends, but also found something... for me? Someone to take care of me? To hold me when I could no longer hold myself? To ease the nightmares that plagued me? I'd be lying if I did not admit that curling up next to Juk was the first decent sleep I'd gotten since the Skulchers took us. Since Delphine and Chunhua's deaths.

And there was no denying that there was *something* between Juk and I. Regardless of how much I fought it or pretended it wasn't there. My pulse raced whenever he entered the room; my cheeks heated when his gaze found mine. When was the last time I felt even a fraction like this about anyone else?

I turn over again, lying flat on my back. My mind will not quiet. The moonlight from the two moons outside filters in through the opening and dances across the ceiling above me, before being swallowed by the shadows of the tall cave.

Conceding that sleep will be lost on me, I stand. For what purpose, I'm unsure. I brush the dirt off my pants. The miner's suit I refuse to give up is filthy. The black fabric is matted with everything possible, from bits of frozen ice that refuses to melt, to dust from the rocks and rubble from the cave collapse.

If I'm going to be riding on Juk's back tomorrow, exposed fully to the elements, then I'm going to need to wear something warmer. It's a small step forward of acceptance of my fate here on this planet, but even the thought of giving up my miner's suit, even for a day, makes my stomach uneasy.

Suddenly, there's a loud crackle and pop from the fire. It hisses and snaps, whatever piece of wood its chewing on angering the flames. I flinch, as panic and nausea rolls over me. The sound catches me off guard, and Chunhua flashes before me. The hairs on my arms raise as panic rips up my spine, and suddenly my stomach clenches.

I stumble out of the cave as fast as I can, into the cold night under the two moons. I get as far as I can before the small contents of my stomach comes rising up and out of me, splattering all over the snow. My eyes close as I try to take deep breaths and bring down the panic, but all I see is Delphine in a puddle of blood and Chunhua collapsing next to her.

Despite taking deep breaths, air barely reaches my lungs. The sound of my heavy inhales and exhales are lost as a white noise overtakes everything. *I think this is an anxiety attack* something quiet in my mind whispers to me, barely overheard through the pounding of blood in my ears and the haunting deaths of my crew mates.

Two weeks of trying to hold it together are erupting out of me, like soda in a shaken bottle. I'm shaken by what has happened to us. Shaken by the future I cannot control. And now, any strength I thought I had is failing. It's been tested and tried, and did not pass.

Tears begin to freeze to my eyelids. *Why bother?* I think. Chunhua and Delphine are already dead. The chances the other four survived the crash are slim. They had no seatbelts. Nothing to keep them grounded, to prevent them from bouncing around that metal coffin.

Six dead on my watch. Katie separated, lost in a series of caves with no food. The only thing stopping me from curling up into a ball and freezing to death has been my own stubbornness. But suddenly that stubbornness has been beat down and quieted. Quieted by the white noise, blocked out by the blinding of my frozen tears. Curling up into a ball out here, in the frozen snow suddenly seems like the best idea.

"I couldn't save them," I whisper, one fat tear rolling past my shut eyelids before freezing on my cheek. *Maybe it is time to join them in death.*

A large warm hand lands on my shoulder. I don't register it at first, the feeling lost with everything else within me. But then gentle hands turn me around and pull me in close. Warm, bright teal skin meets me as I curl up against a solid form. Two arms wrap around me, and slowly lower us both into the snow.

And there, curled up in Juk's lap, I begin to sob. Sob for the loss of Delphine and Chunhua. Sob for the four missing in enemy territory. Sob for Katie trapped behind a mountain of rubble, trapped in the darkness. Sob for Gragon 6, my home, from where our lives were interrupted. And sob for myself, for placing all these things on my own shoulders, without ever asking if it was mine alone to bear.

JUK

My arms are tight around Leesa. I hold her close, my hearts pounding as our bodies fold together and we sit in the snow. I make sure her legs are tucked on top of mine, intent on being the only one to sit in the cold white fluff.

The stench of vomit is nearby. I don't know what happened. One minute Leesa was restless in her furs. I watched her from the corner of my eye, pretending to sleep against the wall. The next, she stood and flinched, panic rising off her, causing my Seeker to throb. She rushed from the cave and retched, and I followed.

I do not know much about these hoo-man females. I can only vaguely, at best, try to imagine what it was like to live amongst the stars—among Vekao—only to be thrown from them. It must be frightening.

But despite their challenges, the fear they have for their missing companions, they have all been strong. The alpha's mate was clouded with confusion at times, and Leesa and Kay-tee have permeated a subtle fear. I can only imagine what Brex is dealing with at the den with the sullen, dark-haired female.

Leesa is the strongest. It is obvious to anyone who sees her, the fire in her dark eyes, the command in her voice. Though they claim they have no leader, Leesa is like an alpha to her people. And so I know, deep in my hearts, that to see her sobbing like this.. for her to curl up into my arms and let it all out, something is very wrong.

And so I hold her. I hold her as her tears soak my shoulder, a river of them running down my chest. Her body shakes with each one, like the earth did beneath our feet just this past morning.

The moons shift in the sky as the hours pass. Leesa stops sobbing. The tears on my shoulder have dried, and she lies still in my arms. My legs are numb from sitting in the same position for so long, my broken tail lightly throbbing behind me.

I do not dare disturb her. I will gladly sit like this for the rest of my life, if it lets me hold her. At some point, I start to lightly stroke her long black hair. It is silky between my fingertips, smoother than the hair on my own head.

Leesa sighs and shifts in my lap. I was unsure if she was sleeping, but she is awake. Her hand curls against my skin, petting me softly on the chest. My skin tingles at her touch, her delicate fingers whispering across my collar bone. My cock twitches, my Seeker flashing as desire ripples through me. My hands itch to tilt her chin up so I can lick her cheek. Or to press my lips against hers, a strange custom I have seen the alpha and his mate do. I wonder if it is a hoo-man tradition.

But I keep my hands where they are. The fact that she is in my lap brings me happiness alone. There is no telling how long this moment will last, and I will not ruin it by risking for more. *She does not want to stay here,* I remind myself. And yet, she chose me for tomorrow's travel. She chose me for warmth the other night. And she has not refuted my comfort in the last few hours.

"Kay-tee will be safe with Hazen," I say at last. My words are hoarse, dry from the cold night air. But I hope they bring her comfort. "They will make their way back to the den. He will take care of her, of this I can assure you."

"It's not just that," she whispers quietly after a few heartsbeats.

I wait for her to continue. My fingers continue to stroke her hair, and my good tail wags slightly from side to side at the prospect of her opening up to me. *Perhaps I can change her mind... and make her want to stay.*

When she does not say anything more, I prod her. "Do you wish to speak about it?"

Leesa shifts uncomfortably. Her hands stop moving across my chest and I hold my breath. She stiffens in my hold, and finally, speaks in a hushed voice. "I've failed them."

My arms tighten around her. "There is nothing you could have done about the cave," I murmur. "The earth's shaking was out of our control."

Suddenly, Leesa rips herself out of my hold. She stands, her petite form towering over me. At this angle, her small teats are lined up perfectly with my face. My Seeker shines, but I ignore it. Ignore the longing to bury my face between them, to pull her back into my lap and nuzzle her face. My good tail swishes happily behind me, the limp one in pain as it tries to follow, but I push the thought behind me.

Leesa stares down at me, her eyes ablaze and shining with tears. Agony is written on her face, and I want to lick it all away. A whine instinctively tries to escape out of me, but I force it down. I do not like seeing her like this. But I sense, at last, she will tell me what plagues her. What keeps her up at night and makes her wretch into the snow.

"It's not just Katie," she says, tears streaming down her eyes. "It's the others too—they're missing. I can't protect them out there."

I stand, my bones creaking as I do. My tail aches at the movement, throbbing in pain, but I reach down and wipe the tears from her face. My hands cup her cheeks, her skin cold beneath my palms.

"We will find them," I say confidently. "Even if they are in Stygian territory, we will get them back."

Leesa shakes her head. She tries to gaze away, but I hold her in place. My eyes will not leave hers. Not until I can assure her and remove some of the sadness from her eyes.

"They could already be dead," she whispers. "Like the others."

My Seeker flashes and a ripple runs through me. *Like the others.* "What others?"

Her eyes close. Silent rivers of tears run down her face, pooling against my fingers. I brush my thumb lightly against her skin, waiting on bated breath. If there is another group of her people out there, or bodies who need a proper burial..

"My crew is a group of eight," she starts. Her breath hitches as more tears spill from her closed eyes. Ever so slightly, she leans into one of my palms, embracing the touch.

"When the Skulchers came for us, we were working in one of the mines. We'd just found a big score, and decided to work late. I decided... I made the call. I'm the reason we were there later than we should have been, giving them the opportunity to.. to take us," she explains. "One of the miners went up to the surface to unload, and the Skulchers were waiting. She screamed, but we didn't hear her until it was too late—until she was running back through the tunnel, bleeding out. They shot her in the back.

"Once they came into the shaft for us, our medic tried to reach for the injured miner. The Skulchers reached out and snapped her neck. And I just stood there, unable to do anything. I couldn't protect them."

Leesa starts to sob again, and I pull her into my arms. She is so petite, my mate, so fragile. The top of her head only comes up to my sternum. Her body shakes with her sobs, and once again I stroke her hair, relaying her words. She has lost two of her pack already, both of their deaths in front of her eyes. One by blood, and the other by—

Suddenly my Seeker flashes. I think back on when I first saw Leesa, how she flinched ever so slightly as one of the Snowscapes shifted outside. I thought it disturbed her because it was unnatural for her people. But both Ee-vee and Kay-tee have grown accustomed, or so it seems, to the shifting. But Leesa always flinches if she hears it. Hears the snapping of bones.

"That is why you do not like it when we shift," I murmur aloud. "It makes you think of your packmate's death."

Leesa nods her head against my chest. Her arms cling tight around me as her breaths heave. "It sounds just like her neck snapping. It haunts me, Juk. I couldn't save her. I couldn't save

Delphine or Chunhua, or Katie. And there's no telling if the others are alive. I've failed them! I've failed my crew!"

My thumbs move the tears from her cheeks as I stare into her eyes. Glossy and dark, Vekao and Jaci are both illuminated within the depths of the dark brown of her eyes. It is like looking up into the night sky. They hold so much pain and anger, her eyes—and fear. My mate is afraid. Afraid of both what has happened in the past and what the future may hold. Afraid of not being able to control what is coming for them—for her and her pack.

"You have failed no one," I say, confident and unwavering. She starts to shake her head, but I hold it still, the gaze between our eyes unbreakable. "I have seen the look in your eyes before. You carry the burden of being an alpha."

Leesa opens her mouth to protest, but I push on. "You are not the alpha of all the hoo-mans here, but you are to a few. And even an alpha cannot protect everyone. There will be times when an alpha loses a packmate, and there is nothing that could be done. You did not fail them, Leesa. You could not have known that those beings—those *Skulcheers*—were coming. You could not have known that your *sheep* would be torn apart. And you could not have known that the earth would shake and the cave collapse. Some things will always be out of control, even to an alpha."

"I'm no alpha," she whispers.

I shake my head and pull her face closer, leaning down to reach her. "You have the spirit of an alpha. For even when everything is going wrong, an alpha perseveres. Moves forward. Takes the next step to ensure the pack's survival. Is that not what we're doing now? Rescuing the remainder of your pack? Have you not ensured the safety of the sullen one, Melanee, in the den? Did you not lift rock after rock to get to Kay-tee, only ceasing once you knew she was safe? You are an alpha, Leesa. A strong, beautiful, capable female who takes care of her pack. And who I am thankful that Vekao has chosen as my mate."

Her eyes search mine, moving endlessly from one eye to the other. My hearts thump in my chest. I did not mean to mention our mating. The words slipped out before I could stop them, sent out into the cold night air between us. They hang there now, in the air, along with the warm feeling in my thrashing hearts. Air ceases to enter my lungs as I do not dare breathe as I wait. Wait to see if she acknowledges what has been growing between us, that Vekao has chosen me for her as much as she has chosen her for me. Whether she returns to the stars or stays here, that will never change. She is my mate, and I am hers. And only Leesa can decide whether to reject the bond or not.

She does not move. Her breath is as still as mine, her eyes searching for something. My fingers twitch against her face, refusing to let her go. My Seeker shines, but my intuition is blank. There is no sense of what may happen next. And the longer the silence goes on, the louder the thumping of my hearts is. The more I start to suffocate from holding my breath, pleading, praying that she will not reject the bond.

But she wants to go home. Being here is another failure, one she has not voiced. Part of her redemption is to return her pack to the stars. I can sense this. She feels she does not belong here, but I know in my hearts she does. Vekao has brought her people here for a reason. To strengthen the pack. The alpha has found his mate, and I have mine. I do not doubt there are other pairings already in the works. But to tell Leesa this would be to tell her all her pain and misery has been for our gain. And I will never tell her that. Vekao would never be so cruel. *Vekao saved them from a worser fate.*

Leesa looks away and my hearts begin to shatter. *She will reject the bond. She is determined to go home.* And if that is her wish.. then I will help her. I will do anything to make my mate happy, even if it breaks my two hearts into pieces.

My hands drop from her face. I swallow, pushing down the feeling of heartache that threatens to tear me apart. *Fool. You should not have said anything. Should have let it be.*

But as I open my mouth to say something, anything to fill the silence, Leesa's head snaps back up. And before I can react, she reaches her hand up to the back of my neck, and pulls my face down, where our lips meet in a crashing force unlike anything I have ever encountered.

LISA

The minute the word "mate" leaves Juk's lips, something overcomes me. I can't explain what it is. It could be a culmination of my fear and shame boiling together, building to a pressure where it's exploded, leaving only the attraction that has been building up between us the past few days. It could very well be the astrostingents Katie mentioned are in the air, influencing me right down to my cells.

Or it could be because Juk is right. I can't control everything, I can't control what will happen next, whether my crewmates are alive. Who is to say we will even survive getting to the territorial line? Or getting back to the Snowscape den—to even waking tomorrow morning?

And so, with my heart thumping heavily in my chest, with Juk's impassioned speech echoing through my ears and whispering to my soul, I pull his face down to mine and our lips meet. Throw caution to the wind, if just for this one sweet kiss, to see what these building feelings are telling me.

The moment they meet, I see stars behind my eyes. Every one of my veins is on fire. My heart seizes, and even though it's clear Juk has never kissed before, it's the best damn kiss of my life. If this is how Evie felt when she first entangled herself with the alpha, then I understand. I rescind my earlier bitter thoughts about her, for the jealousy that she's somehow found a happy ending so quickly in this shitty situation, when my own was right here in front of me.

Juk's arms wrap around me, strong and secure. I melt into them, my fingers curling into the base of his neck. Juk is a fast learner. He matches my fervent kisses, each one sending a shiver down my spine. His tongue sweeps across the seam of my lips, the sensation causing heat to spread to my core. I think it's an accident, as when I open my mouth and my tongue meets his, he groans and grips me tighter. I've seen Axyll nuzzle Evie's cheek and sometimes give it a small lick. Their affections must reside with their wolfish behaviour, carried over into their human form.

He does not hesitate to mingle his tongue with mine. It's incredibly cold, but refreshing. Almost like his entire mouth is a popsicle, and when we part, breathless, my own mouth tingles like I've just sucked on a peppermint.

Juk cradles my face, his eyes searching mine as we pant, breathless. The moonlight glimmers off the crystal in his forehead, the light aquamarine colour lost in the bright teal of his skin. His bright blue eyes bore into mine, and I want to stay here, lost in them forever. To forget all the horrible things that have happened, to let go of the fear and grief, of wondering what the future will bring, and just stay here. In this moment with him, where for the first time in nearly two weeks I feel safe.

"You... you accept me?" Juk whispers. The hope in his voice causes a fissure to crack into the wall I've put around myself. The longing, yearning in his eyes shines down, the hitch in his breath as he waits for me to answer. "You accept me as your mate?"

My heart pounds, the only thing audible in my ears. I place my hand over top of his as he continues to cradle my cheek, his gaze locked on mine. He drops his other hand and places it on my hip. A wisp of his white hair escapes the bun on his head, trailing in the breeze that whiffs by. It runs across his forehead, cleaving the gem in two, but he does not brush it away.

"I don't know," I whisper softly at last. My fingers curl around his as I turn my face away, unable to watch the flash of heartache that crosses his face before it turns neutral. His fingers are so much larger than mine, nearly twice in length. His thumb is lower on his hand, closer to his wrist. My tawny skin looks so different next to his bright colouring, but as I entwine our hands together, it feels right.

And yet, I can't say yes. The word sticks to my tongue when I try to say it. To say yes is to give up. I can't get that thought out of my head no matter how hard I try. The idea of accepting our situation makes me sick. My stomach twists, yet my heart aches. Every beat says *yes, yes, yes*, but...

Juk squeezes my hip. I look back up to his face, the heartache there gone. His eyes are serious, his Seeker glowing with a light I know is not a reflection of the moons. "When you are ready, I will be waiting. I will always wait for you, Leesa. We are mates. It is Vekao's will. You can refuse it for as long as you need, but it is the truth. And I will be there for you until you are ready."

Something in my heart swells. Juk smiles, my cheek still cradled in his one hand, and I place my other hand on his over my hip. Our fingers entwine, and I bury my face into his chest as he holds me close. And for now, it's enough. My storm of emotions rumbles on, moving further in the distance, put aside for another day. A storm for another time, that I know I can weather with Juk by my side.

LISA

DAY 13

The next morning, I wake up feeling calm. For the first time in days, the gloom from the past two weeks does not hang as heavily over my head. Juk is nestled at my side, his warm arms around me. He lightly strokes his fingers through my hair, the only indication he is awake. The fire crackles nearby, the smell of meat cooking beside it.

I lie still, pretending to be asleep. Juk's hand in my hair hesitates, as though he can sense the shift in my breathing. I am not ready to wake up and see the others watching us. Our close bodies, the gossip it will insight. OK, it's not everybody I want to avoid, just Evie. I can just picture the smug look on her face, and it's not something I want to endure right now. Not when the main priority is still retrieving the others.

But I think of Juk's kiss last night, the perfect way his mouth fit mine. The coolness of his tongue, so opposite to the warmth from his body, and the tingling sensation it left down my throat. I wonder if other parts of him are warm or cold, if swallowing him would leave the same tingling sensation...

I squirm at the thought, heat pooling between my legs as my core throbs. *One kiss and now all I can think about are blowjobs. Focus, Lisa. There are seven women depending on you.*

Juk shifts as I squirm. It doesn't help because now I can feel something long, hard and throbbing against my leg. *Warm on the outside but maybe cool on the inside?*

There *must* be astrostingents in the air making me this horny.

"I need to go confer with the alpha," Juk murmurs into my ear. "There is tea stewing over the fire, and some smoked meat set aside for you. The others have been awake for a while, but we will need to get moving soon if we wish to make good time today."

I nod against his chest. He shifts against me, the feel of his cock against my leg disappearing as he stands up. Either he's walking around unashamed with it tenting, or the Celetans can control their urges like a switch.

It takes me a few more minutes to calm myself. I think of Allison, Gabby, Chelsea and Vivianna. We've been stranded on his planet for nearly two weeks now. Two weeks of nothing but endless snow and cold. The three of us barely survived in the bridge. We had mild heat and rations, and an overflowing latrine, but it was something. A shield across the door to protect us. I can't imagine how the seven in the cargo hold are faring.

It sobers me up quickly. The heat rushes from my body, replaced with cold determination. We are almost at the location on the map. Almost at the border of the two pack territories.

I sit up and watch as Juk leaves the cave. His good tail swishes back and forth, but the sight of his limp one cracks my heart. This has not been an easy journey. *Nothing* about the last two weeks has been easy. But it has to get better at some point. And maybe, as I take one last glance at the tall teal piece of meat disappearing through the cave's opening, I already have one thing that will help make it easier. I can see the path it will lead to, and it helps ease some of the trauma away.

It's going to get harder before it gets easier. The thought rings through my head as I stand, and stretch. I settle by the fire and help myself to a stone cup of tea. It's earthy and bitter, but the warmth of it seeps through my body, steeling my determination. Whatever awaits us at the territory's border will be the last hard step towards moving forward, moving on to whatever life awaits us here, with the Snowscape Pack. With Juk.

Evie quietly sits down next to me, her own steaming cup of tea in her hands. There's a glow about her that I see now in a different light. Not one of envy, but of hope. Hope that one day I, too, can be at peace with what has happened to us, to the new life we'll start here.

I clear my throat just as Evie starts, "Things have been tense between us—"

We both pause and I wave at her to continue as I reach for one of the pieces of smoked meat waiting near the fire.

"It's been a difficult few weeks," Evie starts again. "For all of us. Part of me forgets that your group was only on the ship for three days before it crashed. That you all still held hope of being rescued or escaping. I'd been there two weeks already, resigned to... whatever the Skulchers had planned."

A knot forms in my throat. That's right. Maybe Evie accepted sanctuary on this planet so easily because she'd been gone from home for so long. "It's all still very fresh feeling," I say at last.

Evie nods. "And that's ok. Nobody is asking you to pick out a cave and live happily ever after. It'll take a long time, for all of us, to move on. To grieve our old lives, the people we left behind, and to make peace here. Finding comfort—love—with Axyll... it doesn't mean I've forgotten about the others. About the seven women we've been spearheading towards, about Briley and Meg lost out there on their own. I worry about them all constantly—especially Jade. Of all the kidnapped women on the ship, before your group arrived, she was the most fragile."

She pauses, closing her eyes as though she can imagine the mangled cargo hold, or whatever horrors we might encounter in the next day or two. "I know it seems weird to find love in this situation. Love seems to find the worst circumstances to expose itself. But at least now I feel safe. That's the main comfort it brings right now. We can explore where it will take us later, once things have settled. Because despite what you might think, finding the others is my top priority too. Axyll is determined to find the other women and bring them to safety. Regardless if they're in Stygian territory, he sees them as part of our pack—the Human Pack—which he has deemed now part of the Snowscape Pack. We won't rest until we find everybody... or give them a proper burial."

The knot starts to tighten in my throat and I glance towards the cave entrance. I can see a part of Juk's back, and a different blue arm moving in front of him. The Celetans talking about the day's plans.

"It just feels so... *wrong*," I admit at last, turning to her. Her big brown eyes are earnest, her face soft. There is none of the hostility I know I have been throwing her way the past few days, and the guilt starts to leech inside, mingling with the knot in my throat. "To have all these feelings so suddenly when there are many more important things to be focusing on..."

"Nobody can help the way they feel," Evie says. "And those feelings aren't getting in the way of focusing on finding the others."

"I'm just skeptical, I guess," I confess. "Both of us suddenly finding... whatever this is. Mates, by their words. Is it real or is it just something in the air? A pheromone or chemical natural to the planet, forcing us to be together. Have you ever been around a Cloktyl when they're in heat? Once they release those pheromones, anyone nearby is helpless against the lust..."

Evie laughs. "No, I've thankfully never been around a Cloktyl, but I've heard about them." She then tilts her head thoughtfully, and glances at the cave's entrance toward the Celetans. "Even if it is one of the astrostingents in the air that computer picked up on... does it matter?"

Before I can answer, she continues, thinking aloud. "It's not like Axyll and I need to stop and have sex every hour. We're not out of control in lust, needing to mate all the time. It feels like any healthy relationship should, just... deeper. Righter than any other relationship I've ever had." She shrugs and looks back at me, smiling. "I can't explain it more than that, but I think you probably know what I mean. Or you will, if you let yourself. And if it were some pheromone thing, we'd all have been affected by now. Wouldn't we be in orgies? Or wouldn't you be lusting after everyone instead of just Juk?"

She has a point. The only one I have growing feelings for is Juk. And Evie and Axyll are clearly only attached to each other. Yet I sigh and chew my bottom lip. "But what are the chances of the two of us finding 'mates?' They think it's their moon pairing us off."

Evie shrugs as she stands. She downs the rest of her tea and licks her lips. "And what if it is?"

My eyebrow arches, and I can't help but smirk. "You and I both know those are nothing but two moons in their planet's orbit. There's nothing magic or mystical about them."

Again, Evie shrugs. "Who's to say for sure? There are many mysteries out there in the universe. And not all of them can be explained. Sometimes, you just need to believe."

Soon we're off on another grueling haul through the snow. The sun hides behind clouds for most of the day, the chill biting through my suit. Kalpa pulls the large sled, now our only option to carry supplies.

My legs ache riding on Juk's back. By the time we settle into the shelter for the night, I am exhausted. I've done a thirty-six hour shift before in the mines, but somehow this was harder.

It takes all my energy to sit up right in front of the fire and eat dinner before I collapse in Juk's arms for the night.

In the morning, it's another long day. Tabros runs ahead as scout. Axyll runs close behind, Evie on his back. Juk and I are close behind.

I feel miniscule on his broad back. He's wider than the sled. With every movement of his legs, paws barely touching the snow before moving onto the next step, I can feel his muscles work underneath me.

It's not long before my legs are sore from riding. I don't know how Evie got used to this so quickly, but I feel like a duck out of water as I grip his stark white fur with my gloved hands, praying I don't lose balance.

There is something intimate about riding on his back. And something badass. I feel like we're charging into war, and can't help but feel a sense of pride as I glance at the other wolves and marvel at how large Juk is compared to them. I guess I'm the warrior princess now. It's oddly a nice feeling.

Tabros howls ahead, and Axyll starts to slow. Juk and the others follow his lead. Baz runs ahead, another barrier between potential danger and the alpha and his mate.

I glance towards the sky. It's hard to decipher the time with the sun hidden, but I think we've only been running for half the day. *There's no way we'd be there already.* Juk said it was another two days still. Maybe one if we hurry, but there is still at least one night in a cave before we arrive at the border and crash site.

My thighs grip Juk's broad form as I think about tonight. Another night together in the cave, though perhaps with less hesitation. I find I almost anticipate curling up with him next to the fire, wolf or human form. My hand absently strokes his fur at the thought of it, and his large head glances over his shoulder at me.

That third eye finds me immediately, watching me in that soul-searching way.

Tabros lets out another howl, and Juk nods his head towards something in front of us. My attention snaps up at once, my heart racing.

At first I don't see anything. Tabros and Baz are in the near distance, their white forms barely discernable through the snow. The clouds have completely overcome the sun, and I squint, trying to peer past Evie's form as she and Axyll creep closer to the waiting Celetans.

It's when Evie slips off Axyll's back that I see it. My body stiffens at once, all thoughts of Juk lost.

Stark against the white of the snow is a streak of black. At first it looks like a piece of rock jutting out from the snow, but I know the Celetans would not stop for a mere piece of terrain. This is part of the ship.

I practically leap off Juk's back as I catch up to Evie. She kneels in the snow, her hands working fast to brush the snow aside.

I slide in next to her, my knees digging into the snow. My hands shake as I push the snow off the sleek black metal. The Celetans start to sniff around it, digging with their enormous paws. Juk's third eye stays on me the entire time as he moves up to the top corner.

"Has it been snowing enough that it would be this buried?" Evie asks, her voice laced with panic as she continues to brush off snow.

"It has been two weeks since we crashed," I remind her. My heartbeat roars in my ears, a beat to the anxiety running through me. *They're still alive, they're still alive.* It can't have ended like this for them.

"Shit," Evie whispers and she starts to dig faster. "Has it been that long already?"

I sit back on my heels as my fingers grip the lip of the metal. It's about two inches thick and jarred on the bottom.

"Juk!" I call, and he's next to me immediately. He nuzzles me, that third eye watching intently, and he sniffs around me, in a way I know he can't help himself. "I'm fine, but I need you to lift this up."

His muzzle moves from my face to the sheet of metal in the snow. A low, grizzly huff sounds from his throat, and Baz is next to him, the command foreign to me. Maybe one day I'll learn to decipher the different types of gruffs and barks they make. *He* makes.

The two wolves dig under the exposed lip. It does not take them long with their large paws. Juk edges his nose under one side of the corner, and Baz the other. Between the two of them, they lift up the piece of metal.

At first it takes some effort, but as the remaining snow falls off to one side, the sheet lifts easily.

Just as I suspected, it's not the cargo hold. Evie and the others stop digging.

Baz lets the piece of metal drop back into the snow.

"It's just a piece of siding," Evie says, breathless. One of the farther corners is curled up, and there is a long gash down one side.

I stare at the sheet of metal. Though it's heavy because of its size, it's a filmy piece of shit. A wave of anger rises in me, a tide I cannot stop, and I kick the thing.

"No wonder the damn ship broke apart. This is garbage!" I shout. The faces of my missing crew members flash before me, as well as those of the other three women. If this piece of siding ripped off so easily, I can only imagine what was left of the cargo hold once it hit the surface.

"At least it's just a piece," Evie says slowly. I know she is rationalizing the situation to herself. It's her coping mechanism. "And this shows we're going in the right direction."

Axyll nods his head. He's the size of a pony, his eyes level with Evie as she stands again. She pats his head absentmindedly, and he nuzzles into her neck.

"We'll be there soon," she says, looking over at me.

Juk walks over. He towers over me still, even in wolf form. His eyes search mine. I take a deep breath, willing the wave of anger to subside.

Juk lowers his head to me, and I press my forehead against his. The third eye closes, and a calm washes over me. His fur is soft against my forehead. A breath huffs in my face, a silent question.

"Let's keep going."

JUK

As we move through the snow, we find no more pieces of the *sheep*. There is a metallic tang in the air that stings my senses and burns down my nose. There must be smaller pieces buried beneath the snow, none that can be seen by the eye.

All I focus on is the weight of Leesa on my back. She is light between my shoulder blades as she grips my fur for stability. Her thoughts have been quiet since we stumbled across the great shard of black metal.

I can only imagine how she feels. There have been dangerous times before, where a packmate goes missing after a hunt. When tensions were high between the three packs. Rarely does it end in tragedy. We have been fortunate in that regard. The last trying times were when the sickness swept through the packs and wiped out many of the elders.

That was many cycles ago. Since then, times have been oddly at peace. Each pack has respected their own boundary. Fighting among them, scraps and deadly brawls, have not occurred since before my sire's time. Before he passed, he would tell me many great stories of his father fighting against the others, blood splattering the snow.

Is that what will become of this? I wonder. We are nearing the territory border with the Stygians. There is no telling what the brutes will do if they find us wandering close to the line. Or worse, if we must cross it to rescue the rest of Leesa's people.

I am so lost in my thoughts that I miss the instant my alpha pauses.

Axyll's ear twitches. It is minuscule, but the moment he does it again, and his footsteps slow, I pause. Leesa grabs my fur at the sudden halt in my tracks as I turn to look at my alpha. My Seeker shines brightly in wariness as I do. Something uneasy churns in my gut, and then I see it.

The landscape has changed. Though I have not been to the Stygian border in quite some time, I know it like the back of my paw. My tails twitch, my broken one twinging in mild pain as it heals at a crooked angle.

Where once there had been a flat plain, there are now boulders.

I glance up toward the rocky face of the cliff a few feet away. My alpha turns in the same direction. Where normally snow covers the rocky cliffs, it is now laid bare. Mounds of snow, the result of an avalanche, are built up at its base. Black rocks from the mountain's side poke up from beneath the piles.

Axyll turns towards me, his Seeker meeting mine. *The earth shake has reshaped the land.* A soft, warning growl comes from his throat and I nod my head in agreement. This will not bode well for the hoo-mans if they landed near here.

"What is it?" Leesa whispers. My mate is smart, not missing a thing. The alpha's mate casts a nervous glance over to her. "Why have we stopped?"

The alpha huffs loudly this time. The warm air rushes from his nostrils, clouding in front of him. His mate pats his head as she turns towards Leesa. "Something is different here. Perhaps because of the earthquake?"

A bristle of envy runs through me, but it is brief. Already they are so in tune with one another. She understands him in his celestial form despite that he cannot use words to communicate. I long for the same connection between me and my mate. But I cannot be greedy. Vekao will strengthen our connection with time. It has only been one day since Leesa admitted there is something between us. I must be patient. Finding her people comes first. The rest will fall into place when ready.

Kalpa and Baz warily approach the mountain of snow. The metallic scent in the air here is faint but sharp. I cannot describe it as I turn my head, trying to follow the scent and find what peak the sharpness comes from.

Suddenly, Kalpa begins to whine. I snap my head back to him. He abandons the sled, dropping the pulley like it is poison, and starts to dig furiously in the snow. Baz huffs at him in question, but then suddenly his ears go back. He too, begins to dig furiously in the snow, and the fur on my back stands on end.

Distracted by the metallic linger in the air, I missed it. The soft scent hiding under the snow. It is faint, but vibrant and fresh.

"What's happening? Is it the ship?" Leesa asks. There is a hitch in her voice and my heart breaks. She worries so much for her people.

I need to help Kalpa and Baz dig. My shoulders twitch as I gently try to wrestle Leesa off, but she grips my fur, not understanding. There's a quick snapping of bones as Axyll barks at Tabros, who quickly shifts. His blue skin is bright against the mound of snow behind him.

"There's someone trapped under the snow," he explains in panted breath. "The alpha and beta need to help dig them out."

Leesa lets go of my fur at once and jumps from my back. Ee-vee does the same from the alpha, and together we race towards the mound.

"Oh my God," Ee-vee whispers. "Do you—are they still alive?"

"It is hard to tell, but the scent is fresh and warm," Tabros explains. The rest of their chatter is lost as I dig with all my might.

My paws scrape against rock dragged down with the snow. The pile is a mix of fluffy snow and black rock. The rock scratches against the pad of my paws and the snow causes my nose to twitch with each deep swipe.

As we get deeper into the pile, Axyll's Seeker meets mine once more and growls darkly. He nods towards the pile and then glances up at the mountain. I follow his gaze and carefully study the curve of the cliffs, the silhouette against the sky. There, I notice it. The curvature and proximity to the territory line. There is a Snowscape cave buried under the snow here.

We focus our efforts towards where the cave's opening would be, and as we do so, the scent becomes stronger. It is hoo-man and female, I realize. Unfamiliar, but those underlying similarities to Ee-vee and Leesa are there.

I snap back at Tabros, a command he will understand to prepare the rescue supplies from the sled.

Leesa and Ee-vee help Tabros in my peripheral vision. The alpha and Kalpa are nearing the entrance to the cave. Axyll turns towards me. He is half buried in the snow, and he nods towards it, barking in two sharp tones. They are near the bottom. As I am the biggest, I must move through first to create the biggest possible opening.

The alpha and Kalpa move aside. As I move past them, I notice Kalpa seems particularly distraught. He whines towards the hole they have started. It tunnels into a black abyss.

Soon, I huff towards him. *We shall free whomever is down there soon.*

The snow sticks to my fur as I hunker down and dig into the hold. The cold tries to seep into my flesh, but my warm fur holds it at bay. The scent starts to grow stronger. It is light and airy; of sunshine. I can describe it no further than that. It is not the strong musk of my mate Leesa, but pleasant enough. I hear Kalpa let out a small yip, and I growl at him to be patient. I need to ensure the hole does not collapse on me.

It feels like an eternity crawling through the hole. Everyone's breath is bated, waiting on me to complete this mission. If one of Leesa's people are down here, I do not want to fail her. Not after she has been separated from Kay-tee. Not when she has lost two of her people already.

Through the abyss, there is a sudden rush of air. The snow breaks away into the cave's entrance. A light glows from within. It is faint and feeble, the weakest fire I have ever seen alight in a pit.

As my eyes adjust in the shadows, the cave looks a mess. Supplies are dumped and scattered. There is no order here, and I wonder if instead of a hoo-man, if a leope or other creature came in here. Perhaps a wild, untamed lupin. Or a vrander, though they do not normally take to caves.

The scent of the hoo-man is strong in here, but my hearts begin to beat wildly. What if we are not hurtling into a rescue scenario, but one of tragedy? What if the remains of one of Leesa's people are in here, a half-forgotten meal by a leope?

It would not explain the flames, my Seeker reminds me, and I take another scan of the room.

And there, cowering in the shadows, I see her. A small, slight frame, shaking from the cold. As I take a step toward her, the reek of feces and urine, of dirt and sadness hit me all at once. It is mingled with her scent.

My eyes lock on hers, and she starts to scream. I am taken aback when the pointed end of a spear comes towards me, but she does not know how to use it. She swings it wildly and weakly, the weight of it too great for her arms.

"S-stay back!" she sobs.

Something bumps into me from behind. Hands push into me, begging me to move forward, and the Ee-vee's scent hits me.

I carefully move to the side, away from the wild hoo-man, and let the alpha's mate pass through. The spear comes too close to her face, and I growl a warning at the female. Protecting the alpha's mate is my duty.

Ee-vee slides into the cave, ignoring the spear's pointed end. She stands up carefully, her arms spread out in a submissive manner, as the wild hoo-man emerges from the shadows.

"Evie?" she whispers, her voice cracking on the name.

"Oh my God," Ee-vee whispers. "Jade."

LISA

It takes what feels like eons for Evie to calm Jade down. At first, she refuses to believe we are real, and I don't blame her. She is nothing but skin and bone. I can only imagine what she has been through, alone and out here on this strange planet.

Imagine is all I can do until Evie settles her. Once Jade believes Evie is firm and real, and not a figment of her imagination or death reincarnate coming to claim her, the next obstacle is the Celetans.

The aliens frighten Jade in both their wolf form—understandable—and humanoid form. I try to recall where Jade is from, if it is Terra or another mostly human planet. It would be exceptionally rare for her not to have encountered another lifeform in this day and age, but perhaps she has been planet bound. Or she is just very jumpy and anxious about everything.

While Evie settles her, and most of the pack shift outside, I shore up the fire. Jade had been trying to burn the food supply instead of the wood, which explains her pitiful fire.

Once it is roaring and the cave is filled with light, her cries and screams have stopped. Evie holds her tightly to her side, and Axyll drapes one of the spare furs around them both. He does so with careful, small movements, as Jade flinches away from him.

Soon the cave is warm and cozy. Kalpa cooks stew over the fire. His blue eyes flick to Jade every few moments with a worried expression. I can't help but fixate on his behaviour. We're all antsy about what she will have to say—about the fate of the others. My skin itches in waiting. I want to shake her and demand to know where the rest of my crew is. But that won't do any good. She is traumatized.

But the look Kalpa gives her go beyond anticipation. The way his Seeker shines when he turns towards her is familiar. It's the same gleam that happens when Axyll is with Evie, and when Juk looks at me. All I can think about now is my earlier conversation with Evie. How she's certain there are no pheromones in the astrostingents in the air, because then we'd be lusting after each Celetan that walks by. About what she's said about how some things can't be explained. Some things are mysterious and are meant to remain a mystery. But if another pairing is happening before my eyes, then... well, I don't know what to think. I don't want to think we came here for a reason, that we were meant to arrive on this frozen rock. I'll never accept that Chunhua and Delphine were meant to die in those horrible ways.

Fate is a strange thing though. I doubt Jade will be interested in Kalpa any time soon. She shrinks away from him as he offers her a bowl of stew.

"Thank you, Kalpa," Evie says, accepting it on her behalf. "Jade, it's food. These people won't hurt you."

Evie's been murmuring the same things over and over for the past twenty minutes. Jade listens quietly as she explains the Celetans and the Snowscape Pack, how Melanie and Katie are alive. She doesn't mention the rival packs or that she's mated with the alpha.

I sit down on Jade's other side. Kalpa hands me a cup of soup and I nod in thanks. I take an exaggerated gulp of it, hoping to prove to Jade that it's safe. It's a bit bland and watered down as we try to save rations, but it's not bad. The warmth from it spreads through me, and I'm pretty sure I've burnt my tongue.

Slowly, Jade takes a sip. As more silent minutes pass, her shoulders start to relax. Evie keeps her arm around her, rubbing her arm comfortingly. Kalpa sits on the other side of the fire, watching Jade. Axyll murmurs something in their native tongue, and Kalpa averts his eyes and instead starts to poke the fire.

The alpha checks the cave behind us. Apparently, this was one of the bigger Snowscape caves in their territory. At one point it had been considered as a spot for a second den, generations ago when the pack was thriving, but the alpha at that time considered it too close to the Stygian territory.

"Jade," Evie says at last. Her voice is gentle but firm. "Why are you out here on your own? What happened to the others?"

I grip my cup as Jade stays silent. Her eyes find the fire, the flames dancing in their reflection. I know the look in her eyes. Whatever has happened is replaying in her mind. I can almost see the horrors of whatever they went through flashing before her eyes.

Jade takes a deep breath and I hold mine. *They have to still be alive. Gabby, Chelsea, Vivianna, Allison. Jade can't be the only one who made it.* But as she opens her mouth, something catches her attention and she snaps it shut.

Juk crawls through the hole. He has been ensuring its stability, packing it with snow and rounding out the edges so it does not collapse. Tabros and Bex will spend the night outside in their wolf forms should we need to be dug out again. And to protect the sled and supplies.

His eyes meet mine at once. I give him a slight nod, assuring him I'm OK. Jade shrinks back as he stands, the full height of him towering. There's a swell of pride in me that I would have once ignored, but now I embrace it. The curve of his muscles, the bright tinge of his skin. I admire all of it as he walks over. He gently places his hand on my shoulder and squeezes it as he walks past to join Axyll behind us. I suspect they're giving some space so as not to frighten Jade.

"That's Juk," I explain. "He's one of the pack's betas."

"H-he's so big," Jade whispers.

I nod. "He's the tallest, yes. All the Celetans are taller than us. But as Evie said, they are kind. They saved us and took us in. And now we're here to save you—and the others." I emphasize the last point.

"What happened, Jade?" Evie asks again gently. "Start from the beginning."

Jade turns her focus back to Evie. Tears brim in her eyes and as they run down her cheeks, they leave clear tracks in the grime on her face.

"T-the cargo hold broke off from the ship," she says, her voice shaking. That blank look in her eyes returns as she remembers. I can't imagine what free-falling in that tin can must have felt like. To my own surprise, I reach out and place my hand on her knee. She glances at me before looking back at Evie. "It was horrible. W-we had barely anything to grab onto. It felt like we were falling forever before we crashed.

"But we all survived, somehow. Vivianna's leg was broken. One of the crates crushed it as the cargo hold flipped on the way down. Allison and Chelsea set it and wrapped it as best as they could. That was the worst injury. Gabby's leg is still in pain, too. None of the equipment works, so we couldn't communicate with the bridge. Raegan would go and hunt food for us, while Allison and Chelsea would keep the fires going and melt snow for water. We set up a camp but argued about sending someone out to go find you guys. We didn't know where to start looking or if you had survived.

"Four days ago, Raegan went out to search. She never returned. And then t-two days ago..." her voice hitches. The tears pour faster down her face. I squeeze her knee, holding my breath. "There was an earthquake."

I close my eyes. The feel of the quake shakes through my memory. The sound of the crumbling rocks, the dust of the rubble left behind. Katie and Hazen trapped on the other side.

"We felt it," Evie says as Jade falls silent. She glances towards me and I sigh.

"Katie was with us," I start.

"D-did she die?"

"No," I say. "She and one of the Celetans were separated from us. Trapped on the other side of a cave collapse. They've assured me—us—that she'll be fine, and that they'll find their way back to the Snowscape's den."

"What happened with the earthquake, Jade?" Evie asks gently to steer us back on track.

Jade's hands shake as she looks back at Evie and gestures towards her, setting the scene. "W-well it was in the morning—as you know. A few of us stepped outside to, you know... do our business. We set up a 'latrine' area in a little hollowed out rock a few feet from the ship. I was the last to go..."

She takes a deep breath and closes her eyes for a moment. The flames' light dances off the tears glistening against the seam of eyelids. "The ground started to shake the moment I stepped outside. Allison and Navi started to run back for the ship. They probably thought it was the safest place to be, as I did. I started after them, but tripped on the lip of the hollowed out rock on my way out. It crumbled apart like a house of cards, and my foot was stuck. I wasn't hurt, thankfully, but... that two-minute delay changed everything.

"Navi and Allison made it back to the ship. The ground was shaking so much, I could barely run straight. And then, suddenly—"

A loud sob escapes her and Evie wraps her arm around her. My heart thumps hard in my chest, waiting. Waiting for whatever terrible ending fits Jade's story. Something horrible has happened, and I can barely contain the anxiety crawling under my skin.

"What happened, Jade? Where are the others?" I ask. I try to keep my voice soft, gentle, to keep it monotone, but it comes out snappish. This whole trip has been to find them. If it was all for nothing...

Evie shoots me a look, but Jade sobs out her reply. "The ground opened up—s-split open right down the middle of where the ship rested. It swallowed the cargo hold whole."

Jade's breath stutters as she sucks the snot back into her nose, her tears uncontrollable. My lungs cease working, unable to take in any fresh air.

"There was nothing I could do," Jade cries, her attention turned to me. As though I would blame her for a natural disaster, one that has already separated part of our group. "One minute the ship was there, on shaking ground. The next it was gone—p-plummeted to the bottom of the newly made gorge."

Any further attempt of explanation is lost. Jade's words turn incomprehensible as her cries become louder and her breaths shallow. Evie holds her as Jade sobs on her shoulder, her own face now white as the snow outside.

Jade's cries turn to white noise in my ears. All I can hear are the screams of the women in the cargo hold as it ripped from the ship during our crash into the planet. They had to experience that freefall again? It was miraculous that they survived the first time. A second would be unlikely.

All at once, I feel light-headed. Maybe it's grief, maybe it's the hard labour of the travel catching up to me, but I sink to my knees. Far away from Jade's cries, I can hear Axyll and Juk speaking together in their native tongue. Their words are quiet, fluid and foreign to my ears, nothing but whispers among the white noise of the cave.

"I need some air," I gasp, suddenly desperate to get out of the cave.

Before anyone can stop me, I race for the snow tunnel. The icy walls bite into my hands as I scrabble out as fast as possible.

This is it, I think. *This is the end.* There is no saving everybody. There is no finding scrap parts in hope of communicating with an embassy or passing ship. We're really stuck here.

Forever.

JUK

My hearts ache as I watch Leesa leave the cave. My Seeker follows her stiff movements as she leaps up from the fire and disappears into the icy tunnel. I long to follow her, but my alpha keeps my attention.

It is a fine line to walk, I am learning. Who comes first: my alpha or my mate? Before having a mate, the answer was easy. But now that I have one, it is not as black and white as I would have once thought.

But I know my Leesa. Even though our time together has been short, I know if I were to follow her out now, she would rebuff me. She has pride, my mate. She will need a moment alone, under the watch of Vekao, to collect her thoughts and sort her feelings. It will be harder to comfort her if she is not ready to share her feelings. She will be too busy denying them, and it will only result in arguing.

No, she needs a moment. And I understand this. As much as my hearts long to follow after her, to wrap my arms around her and let her cry into my chest, she is not ready to do this. Not yet. I know she will be safe outside, as Tabros is watching over the sled and guarding the cave's entrance. He will not let anything befall her.

"This is not the news we hoped for," my alpha murmurs. He crosses his arms as his eyes rake over the hoo-mans by the fire. I follow his gaze. His mate has her arms wrapped around the newcomer, Jay-ed, who sobs uncontrollably. Tears streak down Ee-vee's face, and her eyes meet Axyll's.

"And you've been on your own since?" Ee-vee asks gently when there is a break in Jay-ed sobs.

Jay-ed's answer is obvious to me. I do not need to see her nod to know she has been barely surviving, on the brink of death. Her skin is sallow, and her arms are nothing but bone. It is a miracle she has survived, and I silently thank Vekao for keeping her safe. From the look on Kalpa's face, he is also thankful—very thankful.

Vekao has kept her alive for a reason, as another gift to the Snowscape Pack.

Jay-ed sniffles, her face streaked with snot and tears. She nods her head as she whimpers. "I thought I was going to freeze to death."

"How did you end up in this cave?" Ee-vee asks.

"Once the ship collapsed into the gorge and the ground stopped shaking, I went to investigate. But, I couldn't even glimpse the ship down there. The gorge is so steep..." She takes a deep breath, more tears spilling from her face. "I knew I couldn't stay out in the open. I didn't know what to do. I figured the best thing to do was wait nearby and see if Raegan returned—"

"Right, you said she was missing," Ee-vee sighs.

Jay-ed blinks and wipes her tears away. She sits a little taller as she nods. "Yes. The second day after the crash, she suggested one of us should go out for help and look for food. Allison volunteered to go with her, but she insisted on going alone. She sometimes would re-appear to drop off food and meat, but for the most part she was gone. It's been four days since we last saw her..."

She sighs. I glance towards the alpha. His face is stone as he faces the hoo-mans, but I know what he is thinking.

More of them are scattered now. There may be bodies to retrieve from the second crash site. Hopefully, instead, there are more hoo-mans. More females to rescue and bring back to the safety of our pack. And then there is still the one who landed in Stygian territory, and the other whose survival is unknown.

Add on Kay-tee and Hazen's separation from us, that is too many new females spread out across the territories unprotected. The only ones who are safe are the three with us, and the sullen one back at the den. I wonder if Brex and his cheerfulness have broken her yet.

"Anyway, I found this cave and was able to start a fire, but I guess an avalanche or storm blocked the entrance while I slept. I woke up to complete darkness and thought.. thought this would be my grave."

Ee-vee pulls her in again for a tight hug, and the two of them begin to murmur between each other. She is a good leader, the alpha's mate. She is soft and gentle, a different type of leader than my Leesa. She is gentle like our healer, but without the powers of a Seeker.

Axyll looks over at his mate with a gaze of pride, before turning to look at me. We speak in our Celetan tongue.

"We will need to go and check the gorge that she speaks of," he says. I nod in agreement. "Not just for the hoo-mans, but to see how it has affected the territory border."

"Do you think the Stygians are aware of the shift?" I ask. The last thing I want is to come face to face with the Stygian Pack while my mate is with me. Those beasts would not hesitate to capture all the hoo-mans and take them for themselves. Females are scarce amongst all three of the packs.

Axyll strokes his smooth chin. "It is hard to say. Their den is quite far from here and underground, from what I know. It will depend on if they felt the earth's shaking under the surface."

Those barbarians. Living under the earth, snubbing Vekao and Jaci... just thinking of them makes my blood boil. With any hope, the crack in the earth pulled the hoo-mans further into our territory and away from their clutches—or killed all the hoo-mans by Vekao's mercy otherwise.

"What is the plan?" Ee-vee asks loudly. She and Jay-ed look over at us expectantly.

"Tomorrow we will return to the gorge and assess the situation," Axyll says.

Ee-vee bites her lip. Her arm around Jay-ed tightens. She tilts her head, her eyes saying something her mouth does not. My alpha knows his mate and his Seeker is wise. Without even speaking the words, he knows what Ee-vee is communicating.

He clears his throat. "Let me clarify. Juk, Baz, Tabros, and I will travel to the gorge and find the *sheep*. I am sending you and Jay-ed back to the den with Kalpa."

Jay-ed's eyes grow as big as Vekao at her fullest. The fear there is palpable. Kalpa lets out a whine so quiet, I know only the Celetans can hear. Her distress makes him uneasy.

"The rest of us will travel to the crash site and assess," Axyll concludes.

Ee-vee frowns at this. It ruffles my fur—even metaphorically—whenever someone questions the alpha's wishes. Even when it is his mate. While more females for the pack would be a blessing, I cannot help but feel weary about the constant pushback our alpha may face. These hoo-mans do not seem to have as high regard for the pack's hierarchy. It does not run through their veins like a Celetan.

"The other women will likely be nervous and afraid of you," Ee-vee says slowly with caution. Her continued optimism that the others have survived is something to behold.

"There is little doubt that Leesa will want to come with us," Axyll says smoothly. He is not wrong. I can already hear the argument my mate would put forth at the suggestion she return to the den with the others. We have come so far to help her people, she will see them dead or alive.

Ee-vee frowns. She glances towards the tunnel and then back to us. I take a step forward, standing tall. "I will go ask her."

As Axyll moves towards the fire to sit with his mate and discuss their new travel plans, I make my way outside of the cave. The icy walls of the tunnel I carved bite into the warmth of my palms as I drag myself out. It is a tight squeeze for me, even in my ancestral form.

The night air is brisk and refreshing from the stuffy cave. The sky is clear, Vekao's bright presence a welcome sight. Tabros lifts his head as I appear through the tunnel. He snuffs at me and nods his head to my right. I do not need him to tell me where my mate is—I can sense her.

Leesa sits on a small rock nearby. Her breath puffs in front of her quietly, as she stares up into the sky. Her dark eyes scan the stars, the moons' glowing in reflection of the dark pools of her irises.

I am silent as I approach her. She looks so small and fragile in this moment. Her legs are pulled up to her chest, her arms wrapped around them as she stares up. I wonder if she is asking for Vekao's guidance. I know it is unlikely, as the hoo-mans do not share the connection and devotion to her as the pack.

She does not move as I slowly sit down next to her. There is no space left on the rock, so I sit in the snow beside it. My tails keep me warm, providing a fluffy seat. The broken one is sore, but it is bearable.

Sitting next to her, I come up to her waist. Even on the rock, my mate is small. I gaze at her, at her beauty, her fragility. I wait patiently for a sign that she is ready to talk, to discuss this upsetting news. This is not the outcome she wanted. Leesa did not want to be a hero—I know that. This has nothing to do with pride, and all to do with looking after those she loves and wants to protect. She already wrestles with the guilt of losing two of her pack—her *kroo*, as she calls them—and now there is this.

Finally, she lets out a small sigh. It is quiet, but enough. I know she is ready.

"The alpha is sending Ee-vee and Jay-ed back to the den tomorrow," I say quietly. "Jay-ed cannot survive out here much longer and needs proper care from the healer. She is skittish without Ee-vee at her side."

Leesa nods. This is not new information to her so I continue.

"The rest of us will continue on to the territory border and see where things stand. It will take less than half a day to get there."

Quietly, Leesa slips off the rock and into my lap. She does not shiver, but her body feels chilled from the night's cold. I wrap my arms around her as she leans into the warmth of my chest. I push her dark, straight strands of hair out of her face, and tuck them behind her small rounded ear.

"I'm going with you to the crash site," she says at last. This is the answer I expected. I nod and rest my chin atop her head.

We stay silently sitting in company for a while. I do not push Leesa any further to release her feelings. She will do so when she is ready, and I love that about her. Because I am the same way. I will not yield when pushed, only when I am ready.

"Do you... do you think there's a chance they're alive?" she whispers.

My arms tighten around her. I wish to tell her what she wants to hear. To reassure her that everything will be ok. But the truth is that I do not know. And I know Leesa enough that what she wishes to hear is not a false lie. It is not the answer her single heart desires, but it is the truth.

"I am not sure."

LISA

DAY 15

At some point in the night, while the two of us sit outside quietly under the stars, I doze off in Juk's arms. I silently cried for what felt like an eternity at his truthful answer, but it's what I needed to hear. I need to stop kidding myself with false hopes about things—like getting off of this planet, of finding all the others alive...

It was miraculous we all survived to begin with. All that we know of—Meg is still uncertain. But now with this news from Jade, all I can think about is Chunhua. Of Delphine. And now, oddly more than anyone in the cargo hold, all I can think about is Katie, And how I have let her down.

She is counting on me to find the others, to find Allison. Allison, Gabby, Vivianna, and Chelsea... while I worry about them, they're resourceful. They can take care of themselves, when needed. But Katie, she is like Jade. Maybe not as much, but she relies on her twin. And now all I can think about is having to tell her, face to face, that Allison is either dead or stuck at the bottom of a gorge in enemy territory.

That is, if Katie even makes it back to the den alive. She's out there, on this frosty, horrible planet, alone with an alien stranger. Evie and I made have found mates—something I am still grappling with—but that doesn't mean there's one out there for all of us. Right?

These are the thoughts that plague me in my sleep. I dream of watching the cargo hold fall into the gorge. I dream of Katie being crushed under the rocks in the cave-in. I dream of her crying, and screaming at me for not saving Allison. For not saving Chunhua and Delphine. For not being smart enough to protect us from something like this.

Later, in a daze, we must have gone back into the cave. I wake up warm by the fire, snuggled up against Juk. Vaguely I remember sliding back down the icy tunnel, exhausted both emotionally and physically from this so-called rescue mission.

The fire at my back crackles as someone stokes it. Soft voices murmur over the sound of the embers. It sounds like Evie and Axyll, quietly discussing the discourse for the day. Today, we split up again. Last time, with Katie, it was unintentional. Jade needs medical attention, which she will not get here. Not in this cave, or even in the Snowscape den—not medical attention as we know it. But she will be better cared for there. Evie will look after her, and with the help of the healer, whose name escapes me, she'll get better. And then she too, will have to come to the conclusion that we're never leaving this planet.

I lie quietly in Juk's arms, his large chest rising and falling as he sleeps. I don't want to socialize with the others yet. I'm not ready to face this day and what we might find at the gorge. What we might not find. There are too many possible outcomes at this point. The thought of any of them makes my head spin.

So instead, I focus on Juk. Of the feel of his right arm curled around my back, keeping me close to his chest. Of the feel of his left arm, heavy and muscular, draped on top of me. It's like a teal weight blanket, making me feel secure and safe. Calm. A feeling that has been fleeting these past few weeks.

My head rests against his shoulder as I watch the rise and fall of his chest. During the night, my leg crept up and wrapped itself around him. Combined with the feel of his arms around me, the heat radiating off his skin and the warmth of the fire behind me... this feels nice. It somehow feels familiar, like this *is* where I'm meant to be.

He is quite handsome, for an alien. There are different species in the Gragon Belt that have made themselves home there, some for generations. I'm not new to seeing alien species, both those who are considered anthropoids and compatible with humans, and those too different. I've had friends of different varieties. I've been attracted to and briefly dated others.

But Juk takes the cake. His jaw is square with sharp angles, and high cheekbones. He has long, blonde eyelashes that match the hair on his head. Asleep, he has his usual scrap of leather out of his hair and the long tendrils fall free from their usual bun. I didn't realize just how long his hair was, as it tickles my face as I crane my neck to get a better look. It falls to his shoulders, a bit longer than the alpha's. It might be a bit longer than mine as well.

I shift my gaze back to his face, to his lips. My own tingle at the memory of our last kiss. What would it be like to kiss those lips now? Without tears pouring down my face, without the stress of the others and our situation weighing down on me. Just a kiss because I wanted to. Because I find myself falling for this man, despite how hard I've tried to ignore it. I gave Evie such a hard time about it, but she's right. There's something here, at least for the two of us. Who knows how many of the other humans will pair up with the pack.

It's unexplainable, but that's OK. Some things don't need an explanation. And maybe by searching for one, by trying to blame it on astrostingents, it may ruin whatever this is budding between us.

Out of my peripheral vision, I see shadows moving around. A timid female whisper joins Evie's, and I know Jade is awake. I feel like I should join them and help them prepare for the day. But I just want to lie here a little longer, tucked into Juk's arms. They don't try to rouse me, which I appreciate.

I place my hand flat against his chest and shift my head so it rests next to it. The deep sound of his lungs breathing in and out is like the ocean to my ears. I've only ever seen an ocean once, on Gragon 8. It was large and ominous, the black waters casually rushing in and out from a dense fog. That was terrifying, but the sound of Juk's lungs is soothing despite the comparison. It's accompanied by the beating of his two hearts.

I close my eyes and try to see if I can differentiate between the two. One sounds like a human's, the rhythm familiar. The other, from what I can tell, seems to beat faster with a continuous beat, like the ticking of a clock. Together they sound chaotic, but when focusing on one at a time, the sounds are beautiful.

Juk lets out a low rumble in his throat. One of his white fluffy tails at my legs twitches, and his left hand shifts to cover mine. "That tickles," he murmurs, as his fingers still mine. I didn't even realize I had started to stroke his soft skin.

"Sorry," I whisper.

"I did not say I did not like it," he murmurs back, and when I glance up, there is a smirk on his face. He opens one blue eye and looks down at me. Light glints off his Seeker somewhere, the crystal shining. I'm not religious at all, but whatever deity made the Celetans sure made an art out of them.

His fingers slowly start to stroke the top of my hand. I place my palm flat on his chest, feeling the suede-like texture of his skin. No wonder they stay so warm in this wintry place. I wonder if he's soft in other places. I wonder what it would feel like to have that soft texture inside me.

Axyll murmurs something in their native language that I don't understand. Juk's Seeker flares for a moment, before he answers back in a low murmur, his aquamarine eyes not leaving mine. There's a desire lurking behind them. It bores deep into my own eyes, right down into my heart where it beats, sending throbbing, aching need between my legs.

Suddenly the cave feels too warm. Too stuffy, too *crowded*. I wrap my hand in Juk's, my heart beating wildly in my chest. *I want him*. The thought is so bright in my head, it pushes everything else out. The rescue mission, the others in the cave, the hopelessness of being stuck here. It's suddenly so loud in my head, that one thought beating with the rhythm of my heart, the pulsing of my core, that I take in a sharp inhale of air. I've been putting off this desire for so long that it's now demanding I take action. Everything else can wait.

The noise of everyone else in the cave disappears, white noise to my ears. I'm vaguely aware of Evie and Jade crawling out of the cave, of the Celetans following them. All I can focus on is the steady beating of my heart, thrumming in my ears. Every part of me feels like it is on fire under Juk's hot stare.

The moment the cave is empty, Juk's lips come crashing down on mine. The kiss is fervent and desperate, one that has been pent up since the moment our eyes first locked when they rescued us from the bridge.

Juk wraps his arms around me and rolls onto his back. His cold tongue plunges into my mouth, eliciting a groan. Shivers run down my body as my nipples perk beneath my suit. Juk's hands run down the length of my body as my fingers find his hair. It's surprisingly soft, and thick. I would have figured it to be coarse like the fur in their wolf form.

I suck lightly on Juk's tongue, the cold minty-like feeling rushing down my throat. His moan echoes in my mouth, and his hands grip my bottom tightly. I can feel the throb of his erection trapped beneath me, the long length throbbing against my leg. And now I wish it wasn't his tongue in my mouth.

But we don't have much time. As Juk breaks the kiss for a moment, gasping for air, our eyes lock and I know he is thinking the same thing. Now isn't the time for slow and exploring. I can't let the others leave without saying goodbye, but if I don't have Juk inside me soon, I am going to explode. When this rescue mission is over and we're back at the den, then we'll take all the time we want. We can lock ourselves in his hollow—*our* hollow, I suppose it will become—for days if we want to.

Just a few days ago you refused to think of staying here. And now you're excited to have a hollow of your own. It's funny how fast things can change.

Juk's hands run up my body again as I sit up straight, as I straddle his chest. I want to feel his hands on me, to feel that soft skin rub up against my own. Slowly, I unzip the front of my suit. Juk's eyes watch in fascination as the toggle moves lower and lower, pulling apart the thick black fabric. But brief disappointment flashes across his face as he sees the shirt I'm wearing underneath.

I can't help but laugh and lean in for a quick kiss. He growls at me and starts to tug more on the zipper impatiently. With quick movements, I pull my arms out of the long sleeves and lift the shirt off. It lands across the cave, and I have a feeling I won't be putting it back on again. It's dirty and stained, another symbol of my refusal to accept our fate. But it's time to move on. To let it go.

The crystal on his forehead shimmers as he takes in the sight of me. He presses his teal hand against my bare stomach. His palm is warm, and his thumb slowly strokes back and forth against my skin. It's a comforting moment of awe and wonder as he stares up at me with nothing but love. I've never been on the receiving end of such a look, and my heart does a flip.

Then the heat returns to his eyes, and with that, the urgency. His hands run up my body and cup my small breasts. Pleasure courses through me, melting me to my core as his thumbs lightly circle my nipples. I need more.

Quickly, I stand and rip off the rest of my suit. Bare before him, Juk inhales sharply, his blue eyes narrowing with desire. Before he can do anything more, I straddle back over him, and move aside his loin cloth.

I've seen the Celetans naked in my two weeks here. They are unabashed by it. They shift so frequently that it is natural to find one strutting across the cave naked after coming in from a run in their wolf form. I think I've even seen brief glimpses of Juk, but this is the first time I've really taken a look.

It's no surprise he's big. He's the biggest guy in the pack.

No time to be shy, I wrap my hand around his length and he groans at my touch. My small hands can't grip all the way around, the tips of my fingers unable to meet. But his size doesn't scare me. If anything, my mouth waters and my body throbs harder, wanting this beast inside me.

His cock is a deeper shade of teal than the rest of his body. There's no hair here, only thick veins running down the appendage. Three large, soft testicles rest below the enormous shaft, and as I give an experimental pump, my other hand tries to cradle all three. The motion is clumsy, but it doesn't seem to matter as Juk lets out a feral groan, and pre-cum starts to spill down the shaft.

I run my tongue up, catching the trail along the way. Like the feel of his tongue, the pre-cum is cold. It has a slightly sweet taste, like venisa juice from home. I guess I'll never really miss Gragon 6 with this tasty reminder right in front of me. *Juk, you might be very lucky in the head department.*

But not right now. I sit up straight again, and shift my weight over him. His hooded eyes meet mine as I position myself over the head of his cock. It presses against my entrance, stretching it already.

"Leesa," he whispers. "I don't want to hurt you, but I am not sure how much longer I can hold back. I have never mated before."

He's a virgin? OK, I wasn't expecting that, but I am also not surprised. The Celetans don't seem the type to sleep around. Mates are taken seriously, and result in a deep bond. I've seen how love-struck Evie seems despite everything else going on.

"Then let me show you," I say.

Before he can protest, I inch my way down on his cock. My core stretches around him in ways I didn't think possible, and I can feel every throb of his heartbeats reverberating inside me. I feel so full as I slowly seat myself down, wanting to take all of him even if it rips me apart.

Juk's hands grip my hips as I finally settle at the hilt of him. With a slow, rolling motion, I grind against him. The movements do not stay slow for long. They build in acceleration and intensity, as the stress, grief, and torment of the last few weeks comes out of me. Tears stream down my face as I ride towards the release that will free me. The release I so desperately need after everything that has happened. The release that will solidify my future here, as Juk's mate.

Juk starts to meet me with each roll, thrusting up into my core. His abs look fantastic from this angle, and one of his balls slaps my backside with each motion. It can't be good for his broken tail, but that doesn't seem to be a concern as he starts to move with feral ferocity.

As the tension builds and we both get closer to breaking the mounting pressure between us, I take one of Juk's hands and shift it forward slightly. His thumb almost instinctively finds my clit, and his sharp nail digs into it just at the right angle.

I cry out in pain and pleasure, in grief and hope as the tension snaps within me, and stars fill my vision. All thoughts leave my mind and my body takes over. Every little piece of tension floods out of me, and with a loud howl, Juk joins me in release.

His seed rushes into me, both cold and on fire, and I don't bother to think of the repercussions his release inside me might cause. There's no need because, incredulously, somehow over the past few days I have fallen in love with him. I am his and he is mine, and whatever comes from that is welcome. I'm not going anywhere.

Juk

I have never known true happiness until this moment. My hearts beat wildly as Leesa lies on top of me, panting just as heavily. My good tail thumps next to me, the motion out of my control. My limp one tries to follow, pushing through the pain, but it is pitiful in comparison. Any smile or feeling of joy before mating with Leesa pales to how I feel now. Now, I feel whole.

Leesa's finger swirls absentmindedly on my chest. The feeling is sensual and content. I wish to lie here forever next to her, to freeze this moment in time. But we both knew this was meant to be quick.

When the alpha murmured to me that my mate's aura was basked in pink, with arousal, it only solidified what I knew.

What I could smell in the air, what made my cock twitch and my heart race. The perfume of it was so overpowering, I could barely respond when he said he would get the others to leave the cave to give us a few private moments. A short time together to consummate and release the tension building between us.

I never expected it to be that intense, though. Not that *good.* Even my wildest dreams could not compare. Even now, as I glance down at my mate lying on top of me, her black hair spilling over one of her shoulders while her tawny skin is pressed against mine, I cannot believe it. I thought it would take endless moon cycles before Leesa truly gave into our mating. And I would have gladly waited for her.

A small sigh escapes between her lips, and she sits up.

"We need to get ready. I need to say goodbye to Evie and Jade before they leave," she says, somewhat begrudgingly. Her eyes meet mine briefly, a furrow between them. Already, her mind goes back to the others waiting, to the endless guilt and worry she feels over the rest of her *kroo*. She is a protective leader, my mate.

"You dress and head outside. I will tidy up the cave and put out the fire, and shift in here," I answer. The sound of my bones snapping will be muffled from the outside, and not bother her with the haunting memories of her fallen packmate.

Leesa is quick to dress. She closes the mysterious black garment that covers her head to toe, and I wrap an extra fur around her shoulders. I do not believe such a thin, flimsy material can keep her warm, and now that we are mated, I hope she will let me fuss over her a little more. I want to take care of my mate, even if she is strong.

With the fur cape wrapped around her shoulders, Leesa presses up on her toes to reach up for a kiss. I cannot help but chuckle, as it does little to add to her height. I wonder, should we be blessed with cubs, if they would have her small stature. Would they have tails? Would their skin be my bright colour or her muted one? What colour would their hair be, and would they be able to shift? All these things would be left up to Vekao, who would know best.

But I am getting ahead of myself. Leesa has only just accepted her fate to stay here with me, as part of the pack. There is no point in bringing up cubs, as we do not know yet if the hoo-mans are able to breed with us. But it is no matter. I will love my mate into an old and cub-less age with nothing but happiness.

I bend down to press my lips to Leesa's. She lingers for a moment, her eyes closing. My scent is all over her, mingling with hers, and it makes me want to howl with delight. This is how it should be, my scent on her. Marking her as my territory, as *mine*. Scenting her so that everyone knows it, and should anyone try to take her away, they will have *me* to deal with.

As Leesa leaves the cave, her crawling up the tunnel giving me a nice view of her backside, I straighten. My back cracks and my tails twitch. Pain radiates through the broken one, though it grows milder and milder each day. I will need to see Nyfer as soon as we return, as I fear it is healing unnaturally. She will probably need to break it back into place, which I do not look forward to. I briefly remember something similar happening to my father, many, many cycles ago.

Once the fire is smothered, nothing but embers dying in the pit, I start to shift. My leg bones snap first, bringing me to my knees as they change their position. Next, my elbows snap and bow out, before straightening backwards. My nose elongates and skull contorts as coarse white fur spurts from all over my body. Finally, my tails grow out in length. The broken one feels a bit of relief in my celestial form. Perhaps shifting more will help it heal properly, and Nyfer won't have to do anything. Transformation complete, I stand. The pain and adrenaline disappear quickly, and I shake all over. The stuffy cave air runs through my fur, and my skin itches underneath. It is too hot in here for my celestial form.

Without a second glance, I bound toward the tunnel, and carefully crawl through its icy walls. The morning's brisk air hits my nose first, and I mentally sigh in relief as I push through the other end. The tunnel is tight around me, my back legs scrabbling to push forward, but I make it out and shake the ice from my fur once outside.

The day is overcast with a familiar grey gloom. Tabros and Baz are in their celestial forms already. Baz snuffs in my direction, and I nod my head at him. He can smell my scent on Leesa and knows of our mating. It will be obvious to everyone in the pack gifted with a celestial scent—which will be all the Celetans and none of the hoo-mans. Or at least, it is my assumption that hoo-mans cannot smell as well as we can. I can't imagine their tiny noses do much.

In the near distance, I can hear bones snapping. Another is shifting, and by the quick glance around, it must be Kalpa. Axyll is nearby, murmuring to Ee-vee and Leesa. Jay-ed sits in the sled. She looks small and frail compared to the piles of supplies built around her.

All that preparation, all those supplies ready to rescue the hoo-mans... and now, those furs may be nothing more than shrouds for their bodies. It is a grim thought, but I pause as I think on it. My intuition does not react. Any thought or glance in the direction of the newly form gorge does not elicit a reaction. Perhaps things are not as dire as we believe them to be. Or perhaps it is too soon for my Seeker to know.

Jay-ed's eyes widen as I walk by the sled. It seems a waste to send all those supplies back to the den when the rescue mission may not yet be lost. But it will be best to know what we are dealing with. Kalpa will return the alpha's mate and Jay-ed, and send the sled back with one of the other deltas. Perhaps

Amble. Something tells me Kalpa will not want to leave while Jay-ed is becoming acquainted in the den.

I approach my mate from behind, and nuzzle her with my nose. I take a deep whiff of her scent by her ear, taking in the smell of our scents tangled together. It is intoxicating. I can still smell our mating on her, the sweat and soot from the cave. I wish to bathe in it, to drink it until there is nothing left for anyone else to detect.

Leea squirms slightly from the affection, the movement so miniscule only I notice it. She reaches her hand up and pats my muzzle.

"Be safe," Ee-vee says. She pulls Leesa into an embrace, and for a moment, it looks like my mate will not return the affection. But her arms wrap around Ee-vee's taller frame, and she grips her fiercely. Whatever quarrel was between them a few days ago seems to be forgotten.

"You too," Leesa says. "Keep an eye out for Katie on your way back."

"She is safe with Hazen," Axyll reassures her, and offers her a pat on the shoulder. I know he is my alpha, with a mate of his own, but in my newfound state of mated bliss and possession, the tiniest of growls releases from my lips at the contact of his hand on her shoulder. Leesa is mine, not his.

Axyll chuckles as his eyes turn to mine. One of his brows lifts, an amused smirk on his lips. I am being ridiculous. He knows this. I know this. It is instinctual, a growl I did not even feel coming. If he were not alpha, he would feel the same way if any other male touched his mate. But he is the alpha. No one would dare do such a thing, should they wish to be exiled like Joval.

As though to prove my point, Axyll scoops Ee-vee into his arms. She smiles and laughs as he carries her over to the waiting sled. Their kiss is long and lingering, and Leesa makes a face and turns away.

"PDA much?" she murmurs to me. The words are foreign to me, and yet I understand her meaning. She is uncomfortable with such broad shows of affection, yet she reaches up and scratches behind my ears as she watches them, disgusted. Little does she know just how intimate the touch is when a mate is in one form and the other in the other.

Her touch is soothing and affectionate, and I nudge my head into her hand, demanding more when she stops. She chuckles now, and we stay like this, her scratching and petting behind my ear, as we watch the alpha tuck his mate into the sled.

Soon Kalpa returns from shifting, and takes up the sled's command. The alpha belays one last message of safety and importance to him, and Kalpa nods his head before they take off.

The alpha's mate waves to me and Leesa one more time, and we watch as they disappear further in the distance, soon nothing but a small speck in a sea of white.

As soon as the alpha shifts, we are off. He takes the lead, Baz and Tabros flanking on either side, while Leesa and I stay behind him. She sits atop me, as light as a blanket. If not for the slight pinching of her grip on my fur, I would forget she was there.

With no sled to pull or hoo-mans walking, it takes us no time to get the territory border. The sun is still hidden behind the clouds, but no snow falls on this day. The winds are still and silent, and yet, my Seeker feels on edge.

Axyll slows and all but abruptly stops as we become within sight of the border. I inhale sharply as I come to a stop beside him.

The landscape is unrecognizable. The few trees that spotted the border are all ripped from their spots in the earth. Large roots snake out from the disturbed snow. Beyond, is a forest that leads into the start of the Stygian territory... except now, that forest, that small patch of wood has disappeared. Swallowed into the earth as though it never existed.

The chasm is bigger than I imagined. A wide stretch of darkness now separates our territory from the Stygian's. It is jagged and uneven, as though the frozen ground opened its mighty jaws to show off its teeth.

Axyll glances towards me. His Seeker meets mine briefly, their eye contact direct.

It is right down the middle.

As though Vekao herself carved a line between the two.

He nods at my response. The contact breaks between us, and he returns to survey the new lay of the land.

As my eyes move from one end of the chasm to the other, I spot something poking out from the snow. Leesa stiffens atop me, as though she notices it at the same time. A small strip of black metal. My nostrils flare, taking in the scent of the earth, snow, and cold. And tangled among it all is the familiar metallic scent of the *sheep.*

"Oh my..." Leesa whispers, the end of her expression swallowed by a sharp intake of breath.

Before I can stop her, Leesa slides off my back and races towards the strip of metal. I bound past her, catching up in an instant due to my long legs. I skid forward in the snow and stop in front of the black shard.

My nose digs into the snow as I sniff around it. The metallic smell here is sharp and bitter. There are no other lingering scents, anything else left behind has been swept away by the wind in the recent storms.

Leesa stands next to me. She places her hand on my shoulder, gripping it to steady herself. I can smell the grief and uncertainty on her, and a small whine escapes me.

With a small pat, she kneels down in the snow and picks up the piece. It is thin and jagged, about the same length as one of my legs.

"It looks beat up," she says quietly. A sad, soft chuckle follows, "Though, considering it was a stolen Skulcher ship, all their shit is beat up."

She sighs as she shifts the piece of metal from one hand to the other. The alpha has wandered over now, and sniffs at the piece. His eyes then look to her, diverting to her lead.

A swell of pride rushes through me. The alpha is deferring to my mate. Mine. It is not often that he defers to another's command or move, except for the healer and sometimes the elders. But in this moment, he looks to Leesa. They are her missing people. Her pack, her kroo.

Leesa looks over at Axyll. His Seeker is focused on her and her alone, while he holds her stare.

She lets the piece fall back into the snow and stands to survey the area. With a glance at me, she then turns her attention back to the alpha.

"I think this is a piece broken off from the crash two weeks ago," she starts. She breaks his gaze and looks towards the newly formed cliff, only a few steps away. "It would not have fallen far from where the cargo hold was. And if Jade says the entire thing was swallowed by the split..."

With a steady hands, she points to a spot in front of us. A spot where the snow suddenly disappears into an abrupt cliff carved in the ground.

Axyll nods and slowly moves towards the spot. The rest of us all follow. Leesa walks beside me, her head just under my shoulder. I let her lead, staying a half step behind her.

Once at the cliff's edge, she places her arm on my shoulder again. Another sharp intake of breath as she steadies herself, and together, we dare to look over the edge.

My hearts fall into the pit of my stomach. It is endless, this drop. My eyes lose focus as I try to find the bottom. It is nothing but dark, freshly exposed stone walls.

The earth's wounds look raw and angry. I shake my head, trying to clear my mind and re-focus my eyes. Leesa kneels beside me, practically hanging off the edge of the cliff as she tries to see the bottom. Her hand is gripped on my foreleg, and I ensure my paw is planted firmly to support her weight. I do not need her to be added to this tragedy.

Unlike my eyes, however, my Seeker is trained on the bottom of the pit. It stays unblinking as it slowly searches the ground, focusing as hard as possible. A fine line of snow has littered the ground. The faint white line is all I can see. My Seeker follows it, and by the tilt of the alpha's head, I sense he does as well.

Axyll suddenly chuffs. His eyes glance towards mine, and he nods his head at something ahead of us. His Seeker stays focused on what he has found, and I quickly follow his line of sight.

And there, closer to the opposite side of the chasm, is what looks like something that does not belong. It is hard to make out the shape of it, but it is clear what it is—the *sheep*. The kar-go-huld, they have been calling it. The back half of the *sheep* that we rescued the others from.

From up here, it is impossible to tell what kind of condition it is in. It looks nothing more than an extraordinarily large boulder, perhaps dented on a few sides. I can make out no hoo-mans or creatures around it. They would be too small to see from up here.

I let out a small noise, a cross between a whine and a gruff, and gently nudge Leesa with my snout. She pulls back from the edge and her dark eyes glance up at me. Air puffs out of my nostrils as I snuff and gently nudge her head towards the *sheep*. She watches me closely, my Seeker specifically, as she trains her own eyesight. She is so smart, my mate. It takes a few times of careful watching to follow my Seeker's trail, but then it happens. She gasps and stands abruptly next to me.

I can hear her heartbeat thumping in her chest. It is strong and frantic, and worry etches across her face. Her features mimic the seedy feeling slowly growing in my stomach as my Seeker darkens. I do not know yet what it means, but I have a very clear idea.

Without warning, Leesa suddenly cups her hands to her mouth and shouts into the gorge, "IS ANYONE DOWN THERE?"

Axyll's head snaps up at us, his eyes glowering. He lets loose a low warning growl, but it is too quiet for Leesa to hear. It is for my ears only, for me to get her to be quiet. Yelling into the chasm is dangerous. Not because of potential avalanches, but because of where we are.

Because the broken *sheep* lies on the Stygian's side of the border.

As Leesa's words echo down, down, down into the fissure, everyone holds their breath. Leesa for a different reason than the rest of the pack. We wait, my eyes now scanning the distant horizon for any movement. For any sign of the black wolves that prowl the now clear divide of our territory. But the snowbank and the distant trees stay quiet. No dark silhouettes appear, yet I continue to hold my breath.

And then, ever so quietly—nothing more than a whisper on the wind—there is a response. It is so soft, and feminine, that at first I feel I imagined it. My Seeker stays dark with worry, a warning that something bad is soon to pass. The Stygians, likely, I fear.

"...ello...?"

The soft voice, the question reaches the top of the cliffs, and Leesa all but collapses onto the ground. Tears fill her eyes, and she grips my foreleg again, and before I can stop her, she cups her hands again and shouts back into the void. "WE'RE COMING TO GET YOU! HOLD ON!"

I turn my gaze to Axyll. Our Seekers stay trained on the sight below, now moving to calculate how we might be able to get down. Quickly, safely, and without the detection of the Stygian's. The alpha's eyes meet mine, and though we cannot communicate through the properties his Seeker as alpha bestows upon him, the meaning is the same between us. It does not need to be said aloud.

They're alive.

Epilogue

Lisa: Day 18

"You must eat," Juk says as he sits beside me. A cup of broth and meat is in his hands, and he all but shoves it under my nose. I try to shoulder him back, but he insists. The stew sloshes inside the carved cup, threatening to spill and I sigh. I don't want to waste food, but I don't want to waste time either. "You cannot help them if you have no strength."

Reluctantly, I put aside the leather straps I've been weaving together and take the bowl of broth. I start to sip down the sloshy stew as fast as possible, but Juk takes it back from me and shakes his head. "Too fast, and you will make yourself sick," he reprimands. "Leesa, you must..."

"Must what?" I snap. His brows pull together, and I take a deep breath. I close my eyes, and take another. He's right. He knows he is, and I know he is. I need to... I don't know. Relax isn't the right word. I need to be levelheaded, but I am finding it difficult. "I'm sorry."

"There is nothing to apologize for," Juk says. He hands me back the cup and then sips from his own.

I take another sip and this time, try to savour it. The flavour is... interesting. It's bland in that there are no spices, no added flavouring that the Celetans normally tend to use. But it's rich, because in this particular stew-soup-thing, Juk drained the animal's blood and stirred it right into the soup. If they've been doing this the whole time, I wasn't aware of it. We're low on food—for now—and need to make use of everything, more than usual. The Celetans already don't waste anything, but making food stretch is something else entirely.

There is so much to be done. Ever since we found the cargo hold's wreckage, my brain has been *go go go*. I'll never forget the sight of the ship down there. From up here, it's nothing more than the size of a pea. I never would have seen it without Juk steering me in the right direction. And when that voice answered...

I close my eyes, replaying it in my head. There's no telling whose voice it was, but it was clearly human. In my mind, it is Allison's. But it could be any of them. We could not keep yelling back and forth all day. That was one thing Axyll shut down. Once whoever was at the bottom said they would be waiting, they've stayed quiet. As have we. There was no way to warn them that it would be wolves venturing down there to rescue them. Wolves that turn into muscular, hunky aliens.

A smirk twitches at the corner of my mouth as I sneak a glance over at Juk. He sips his soup carefully, one hand on the ladle keeping the rest of it stirring over the fire. When my mind wants to wander, to focus on something other than the rescue we're in the midst of, I let it. Now, instead of trying to fight it, I let my thoughts come and go as they please. Those at the bottom of the fissure will still be there, even if I take a quick minute to ogle the man beside me.

Juk. My mate. I still can't wrap my head around it sometimes, how this all happened so fast, and just how *right* it all feels. The universe works in mysterious ways, and now that I've tried to stop finding out *how* it works, I can enjoy it. I try not to think too far into the future. Someday, I like to think I'll still see Gragon 6 again. But that might not be until I'm old and frail. And that's OK too.

When Juk catches me looking, he smiles. A tendril of his white hair has fallen out of the bun on his head, and he flicks his head to brush it out of his eyes. The crystal on his forehead shines in the light of the fire, but I know it shines for me too.

Right after finding the wreckage, the Celetans fell into action. Axyll ordered Tabros and Bex to find a way down. I was adamant about climbing down too, but Juk shut that down immediately.

"It's not even safe for them," he said. "Until we can find a path down, one that ensures a way back up as well, then we can reconsider."

I was annoyed by that and still am. I want to be down there. *Need* to be. I need to know who is down there and in what condition. Were they separated during the crash? How many didn't survive? *What is the status of my four other crew members?* I know there were more than just the four in the cargo hold. Jade, Raegan, and Navi were there as well. Jade's on her way back to the pack now, and she said Raegan had been missing a few days. That means the only people down there are my four and Navi.

My thoughts toss and turn as I stare into the cup of soup. "Does the blood give it extra nutrients?"

Juk nods. "Yes. It will help strengthen the females once we're able to find them."

There's something distant in his voice. It's quiet, and his head tilts away from me, listening for something I cannot hear.

It's his premonition thing. I don't know how to describe it aside from that. The Celetans believe that each Seeker is gifted to them from Vekao. And each one is given a different ability. Axyll can read the moods, or auras as they call it, of other people. Apparently, the alpha can also communicate mind-to-mind with someone in wolf form, but only when their Seekers are directly aligned with each other. It is a skill only the alpha inherits.

Juk's power seems a bit hokier. He can also tell when someone is troubled or worried, but he can also sense when something bad is about to happen. Like the earthquake a few days ago. He can't always pinpoint what the upcoming problem may be, but he always puts a "feeler" out whenever they are about to embark on a particular mission or run. I don't bother trying to understand it, as I've seen some alien species do weirder shit.

We've been cooped up in this cave, different from the one we found Jade in, for two days now. It was the closest stocked hunter's shelter around, and is our base now for the rescue. It's about a half-day's run from the crash site. The cave is large, with two different spaces. A big communal space, where Axyll sleeps. Then there's a smaller cave space in the back, where he lets Juk and I have some privacy. It's not entirely private, but I do my best to keep quiet during our intimate moments. Though the first time I gave head to Juk, I'm surprised the cave didn't collapse from how loud his howling was.

"What's wrong?" I ask. Juk glances over at me and shakes his head. But his lips are in a thin, pressed line, and his nostrils flare. "Juk. Tell me. I know your Seeker is acting up."

His lips stay taut together and he avoids my eyes for a minute, before he sighs and looks back down at the soup.

"Something... something bad is coming. I have felt it since we found the fissure two days ago. I did not want to worry you."

I grip the cup in my hands, my heart already racing like crazy. "Does it have to do with the survivors down there?" My voice has turned into a whisper.

"Yes," Juk answers. He's at least always honest with me. Even if he tried to hide this to keep me calm, I don't count it as lying. He knows how upset I've been and anxious I am to get the rest of the Gragians back together. Hell, it's been my whole personality since we crashed here.

"Is it the Stygians?" I ask. I'll never admit to him that I am a *little* curious about the other two packs that live here. Juk seems indifferent about the Ashen Pack, but the Stygians.. I can practically see the steam coming out of his ears anytime they're mentioned. How different can they really be?

The muscles in his shoulders tense, and his grip on the ladle looks like it might snap the thing in half. "I cannot tell. If it is the Stygians, it is very, *very* bad..."

"And what constitutes as very *very* bad if it's the Stygians?"

He hesitates for a moment, tilting his head once more. His Seeker shines but it is dull. Not the same shine when it's focused on me. "If it is the Stygians, it feels as though the entire pack is on its way. That's how bad it feels. But, I do not think the entire pack..."

I take another large gulp of my soup, waiting for him to continue. He seems distracted again, this time his nostrils flaring. I finish the rest of my soup, and pick up my leather project again. We've been stocking up on supplies here, trying to set it up as a medical base. I've been weaving slings together and makeshift bandages. Juk goes out to hunt animals and check traps, stocking up on food and bringing back furs and leathers to be worked. I've gone through most of what was already supplied here, and have the new hides stretched and drying, working with scraps now until I can do something with the fresh ones.

Axyll goes to the cliffs every day and checks on the others. Finding a way down has been torturous. The rock is too sharp and narrow in most places. But, finally yesterday afternoon, Axyll reported that Tabros and Baz were able to find a way down. It was a few feet away from the wreckage site, but something. They were slow to go down, but he was certain they would reach the bottom by nightfall. Today is supposed to be an update on if they made it down safely and are with the women. My eyes have been fixated on the cave's opening all day. I'm dying for the alpha to come back and report that everything is going to be OK.

"Entire pack what?" I finally prod after a few minutes of silence.

Suddenly, there's a light tremble throughout the cave. *Not another one*, I think, bracing myself for an earthquake. My eyes go to the ceiling, trying to survey if it will rain down on us like before. I can't help but eye all the hard work we've done the past two days and pray that the cave stays intact, solely to not have wasted time and resources.

Juk reaches out to hold me. His large, warm hand rests on my shoulder, gripping it as though he's ready to yank me out in a moment's notice. I look up at him, and his eyes are frantic. His Seeker shines brightly, and I hold my breath. Whatever his intuition was warning him about, this is it. I've been studying his Seeker and its various shines, and this is a new one. This must be it. And he's right—it isn't the Stygians.

The tremors feel different than an earthquake. As a matter of fact, as I look back up at the cave's ceiling, they seem to be coming *above*. And that's when I hear it—the quiet rumble of an engine.

I feel every bit of colour drain from my face. Juk hears the rumbling too, his eyes snapping to mine. We both jump to our feet, him to usher me into the back cave, me to rush to the cave's entrance. I need to see who it is.

I evade his grasp and rush to the cave's entrance.

"Leesa! It is not safe!" Juk hisses at me. But he knows better than to pull me away. Even though he could easily toss me over his shoulder and drag me to the cave, he doesn't. This is outside of his element.

I stay just inside of the cave's lip and watch as a ship flies low overhead. It almost skims against the mountain's rock, but narrowly avoids it as it moves further away.

Just then, a flurry of white runs up to me. It barrels inside, and I wince as bones crack quickly, the quickest I've ever heard. It's the first time I've seen one of them shift up close, but my mind isn't given time to process it. Axyll doesn't even pant, doesn't even take a breather before he's standing next to us, pulling me back further into the cave.

"We saw it coming," he says. I can hear the fear in his voice. Juk stiffens at the sound of it.

"We?" he asks.

"Screks has been following us. Tracking and trailing from a distance," Axyll explains. "I told him to stay hidden and discreet. I wanted him nearby in case we had an emergency and needed backup from the pack. But now that Kalpa is already on the way back, as is Hazen, I've changed his directive. He's run ahead to go and warn the others. With his small stature, he will be quicker to reach the bottom than Tabros and Baz were."

"So they made it to the bottom?" Juk asks. Axyll nods, and the two of them turn to watch the ship shrinking in the distance once more.

I feel like I should be angry that Axyll knew Screks could reach the bottom of the cliff easily, but didn't send him. The old Leesa would have reamed him out, but the new Leesa knows, no matter how much I push and shove, the pack comes first. As a whole. And, as it turns out, it was for the better. Maybe Screks can get there in time and warn them. But something in the pit of my stomach doesn't agree.

I turn away from the black dot of the ship as it nears the cliffs. My stomach twists and I reach out to brace myself against the cave's cold, stone wall. My mouth dries and my legs feel like they will give out at any moment. Fear sinks its claws into me so deep that I don't need to follow the ship to know where it's going. To know what it's after. And I don't need to look twice at the shotty siding, the sleek but dirty black walls to know who it belongs to.

It's the Skulchers.

They're back.

A NOTE FROM THE AUTHOR

Heyo everybody! Thank you for taking the time to read Lisa's story! I hope you enjoyed it. If this is your first time here, I'd recommend heading back to the beginning to read Evie's story.

Lisa's story was difficult for me to write. Her story is a journey, one to acceptance of the past and acceptance of a future she does not want (at first). It's hard to write a character who is so opposed to the ending you have for her *insert obligatory millennial "lol" here*.

Now, you might be wondering: where are we going from here?

The vague answer: Everywhere. We know *someone* is alive at the bottom of the gorge. We need their story. We know Briley is alive out there somewhere. We know (if you've read the short story CELESTIAL RESCUE) that Meg is out there. We have Evie and Jade heading back to the den, where Melanie has been for at least a week now. And we know... the Skulchers are back.

The specific answer: Melanie's book is coming next. It's always been planned that way. While Lisa's was more plot-moving, Melanie's book will be cozier. We'll come to understand what in *her* past has made her so cynical, and we'll learn a lot about life with the Snowscape Pack!

Stay tuned!

THE SNOWCAPE PACK

Here are the pack members of the Snowcape Pack, and the thirteen women as we know them so far:

ALPHA

*A**xyll** (AXE-eel): Snowscape Alpha. Brother to Screks, the omega. Nephew to Mika and Joval, and cousin to Juk, Brex, and Tabros. Newly mated with Evie. Seeker gives him the ability to read the mood of others, and can communicate one-on-one with another packmember when in celestial form if Seekers make direct eye contact.

BETAS

Juk (JOOK): Snowscape Beta A. Tallest of the Snowscapes. Nephew to Joval. Cousin to Axyll and Screks. Born as a singleton. Recently mated with Lisa. Seeker has the ability to "feel" for things about to happen in the future. Currently in a shelter with Lisa and the alpha as they attempt to rescue the other women in the gorge.

Brex (BREHX): Snowscape Beta B. Always in a good mood. Parents are Mika and Vek, and brother to Tabros. Nephew to Veela, and cousin to Axyll, Screks, Hazen, Baz, Riiza, and Tygen.

DELTAS

Hazen (HAY-zen): Snowscape Delta A. Son of Veela, and brother to Baz. Nephew to Vek and Mika, and cousin to Brex, Tabros, Riiza and Tygen. Currently with Katie, separated from the rest of the Snowscape Pack due to a cave-in.

Kalpa (kal-PUH): Snowscape Delta B. Son of Kinna, and brother to Jenneka. Cousin to Nyfer and Amble. Currently heading back to the den with Evie and Jade.

Amble: Snowscape Delta C. Mate to Riiza, and father to Vyker, Jovie, and Kipsan. Brother of Nyfer, and nephew of Kinna. Cousin to Kalpa and Jenneka. Uncle to Hexa, Xynder, Heike, Svyxil, and Kazz.

ELDERS

Veela (VEE-luh): Mother to Hazen and Baz. Sister of Vek. Aunt to Riiza and Tygen, Brex and Tabros.

Joval (joe-VALL): Uncle to Axyll, Juk, and Screks. Was the omega of his generation and very resentful of it. Recently exiled from the pack and has a cracked Seeker.

Vek: Mate to Mika. Father to Brex and Tabros. Retired delta. Uncle to Hazen and Baz, Riiza and Tygen.

Kinna (kin-NUH): Mother to Kalpa and Jenneka. Aunt to Amble and Nyfer.

Mika (mee-KUH): Mate to Vek. Mother to Bex and Tabros. Aunt to Axyll and Screks.

HEALER & FAMILY

Nyfer (nye-FUR): Pack healer. Seeker gives her healing abilities. Mated to Hant, and mother to two litters: Hexa, and then Xynder, Heike, Svyxil, and Kazz. Sister of Amble, and aunt to Vyker, Jovie, and Kipsan.

Hant: Mated to Nyfer. Father of Hexa, Xynder, Heike, Svyxil, and Kazz. Often teaches the cubs and pups how to hunt. Littermates no longer living.

Hexa: Nine-year old female "pup." Oldest of her generation. Her litter mate, also a female, died when born. They were a rare double-female litter. Daughter of Nyfer and Hant, and sister to Xynder, Heike, Svyxil, and Kazz.

Xynder (ZINE-durh), *Heike* (hi-KUH), *Svyxil* (sv-IX-eel), and *Kazz* (rhymes with jazz): Five-year old male "pups." Second litter of Nyfer and Hant. They are a handful. Brothers to Hexa.

OTHER FAMILIES w/ LITTERS

Riiza (ree-ZUH): Mated to Amble. Mother to Vyker, Jovie, and Kipsan. Sister to Tygen. Niece of Veela and Vek, and cousin to Hazen, Baz, Brex, Tabros, and Bansk.

Vyker (VYE-ker), *Jovie*, and *Kipsan*: Two year old "cubs." Jovie is the second female of her generation. First litter of Riiza and Amble.

UNMATED PACK MEMBERS

Baz: Son of Veela. Brother to Hazen. Cousin of Riiza and Tygen, and Brex and Tabros. Currently trying to rescue the women in the gorge.

Tygen (TYE-gen): Brother to Riiza. Uncle to Vyker, Jovie, and Kipsan. Cousin to Hazen, Baz, Brez, Tabros, and Bansk.

Tabros (tab-BROSE): Son of Vek and Mika. Brother to Brex. Cousin of Axyll and Screks, Riiza and Tygan, and Hazen and Baz. Currently trying to rescue the women in the gorge.

Jenneka (JEN-ih-kuh): Last unmated female of her generation. Has a tendency to run off from the pack. Daughter of Kinna, and sister to Kalpa. Cousin to Nyfer and Amble.

Bansk: Youngest of his generation. Born as a singleton. Cousin to Riiza and Tygen.

OMEGA

Screks: Snowscape Omega, smallest in the pack. Brother to Axyll, the alpha. Nephew to Mika and Joval, and cousin to Juk, Brex, and Tabros. Currently with the rescue group trying to retrieve the women from the gorge.

HUMAN WOMEN

Evie (Evelyn): The first of the thirteen women kidnapped by the Skulchers. Originally from Earth, galactically known as Terra, where she worked for a delivery company. She is newly mated with Axyll, and is considered one of the leaders of the women. Currently heading back to the Snowscape den with Kalpa and Jade.

Lisa: Foreman of her crew from Gragon 6, a mining colony. Was on the bridge when the ship crashed. Recently rescued by the Snowscape Pack, and eager to find the rest of the Gragon 6 crew. Currently in a shelter with Juk waiting to rescue the women in the gorge.

Meg (Meggan): Mechanic from Terra 4. Was on the exterior of the ship repairing a shield when it crashed onto the planet. Rescued by Kyp, of the Ashen Pack, and is currently in Snowscape territory.

Briley: Also kidnapped from Terra 4, taken before Meg. Was on the fighter pod when the ship crashed, and ejected to safety. Currently in Stygian territory.

Melanie: From Lagusta, an elite sub-moon of Terra 4. Pessimistic personality. Was on the bridge when the ship crashed, and recently rescued by the Snowscape Pack. Stayed in the den instead of going to rescue the other women.

Jade: Kidnapped last before the Gragon 6 crew. Terrified of her current situation. Was in the cargo hold when the ship crashed, and recently rescued by the Snowscape Pack. On the way to the den with Evie and Kalpa.

Katie: A hurrier from Gragon 6. Worked under Lisa's supervision. Twin to Allison. Was on the bridge when the ship crashed, and recently rescued by the Snowscape Pack. Desperate to reunite with her twin. Currently with Hazen, separated from the rest of the Snowscape Pack due to a cave-in.

Raegan: Taken from the fighting pits of Skulkan-IIX. Original home planet unknown. Can understand the Skulcher language. Was in the cargo hold when the ship crashed. Has been missing for four days, according to Jade.

Navi (Navneet): A xenolinguist from Elmina X. Was in the cargo hold when the ship crashed.

Vivianna: A loader from Gragon 6, in Lisa's crew. Was in the cargo hold when the ship crashed.

Gabby (Gabrielle): A timber in Lisa's crew from Gragon 6. Her leg was injured during the escape from the Skulchers. She was in the cargo hold when the ship crashed.

Allison: Driller in Lisa's crew from Gragon 6. Twin to Katie. Isn't afraid to fight back, and is punched out by the Skulchers when she firsts arrives. Was in the cargo hold when the ship crashed.

Chelsea: A hewer in Lisa's crew, one of the six women taken from Gragon 6. Was in the cargo hold when the ship crashed.

About Author

Charlene Pender is a Canadian romance writer, who likes to write in a variety of romance subgenres: sci-fi, fantasy, and contemporary. She lives in the Metro-Vancouver area with her family, small horde of cats, and too many ideas in her head.

Fine me online at www.charlenepender.com
FB: Charlene Pender
IG: @charlenepender.author
Threads: @charlenepender.author
TikTok: @charlene.pender

www.ingramcontent.com/pod-product-compliance
Lightning Source LLC
Chambersburg PA
CBHW050725180626
46814CB00002B/614